序 言

　　繼出版了「中級英語聽力檢定①～⑥」，我們又推出了「中級英語聽力檢定⑦」，為什麼還要繼續出呢？因為聽力測驗需要不斷地練習，熟能生巧，考試時才能迅速掌握答題的重點。不斷地練習沒有聽過的題目，考試才能得高分。聽力的訓練，愈多愈好。

　　建議讀者實際測驗之後，把錯的題目做一個記號，再繼續聽新的一回。複習時，將不會的題目，朗讀一遍，到真正考試就輕鬆了。對於聽力這一項較弱的讀者，可在實際練習後，將整份試題大聲朗讀一遍。

　　平時聽 MP3 練習時，一定要養成「先看選項，再聽題目」的習慣，看選項的速度一定要超前，如果哪一道題目聽不懂，就必須放棄，立刻看下一題的選項，這樣才能掌握答題的重點，及縮短做答的時間。千萬不要等聽完題目，再看選項，否則整個聽力考試，都會失敗。

　　全書共八回，每一回 45 題，分為看圖辨義、問答，以及簡短對話三種題型。讀者在做每一回測驗時，最好訓練自己，在二十分鐘內作答完畢，因為實際考試時間為三十分鐘，讓自己習慣在較短的時間內寫完，考試時會更得心應手。

　　本書在編審及校對的每一階段，均力求完善，但恐有疏漏之處，誠盼各界先進不吝批評指正。

劉 毅

English Listening Comprehension Test
Test Book No. 1

This listening comprehension test will test your ability to understand spoken English. In this test, each conversation, statement and question will be spoken JUST ONE TIME. They will not be written out for you. There are three parts to this test. Special instructions will be given to you at the beginning of each part.

Part A

In Part A, you will see several pictures in your test book. For each picture, you will be asked 1 to 3 questions. For each question, you will hear four possible answers. Choose the best answer according to what you see in the picture.

Example:

<u>You will see</u>:

<u>You will hear</u>: What is this?
    A. This is a table.
    B. This is a chair.
    C. This is a watch.
    D. This is a doll.

The best answer to the question "What is this?" is B: "This is a chair." Therefore, you should choose answer B.

A. **Questions 1-2**

B. **Questions 3-5**

C. <u>Questions 6-8</u>

D. <u>Questions 9-10</u>

E. <u>Questions 11-13</u>

F. <u>Questions 14-15</u>

Part B

In Part B, you will hear 15 questions. After you hear a question, read the four possible answers in your test book and decide which one is the best answer to the question you have heard.

Example:

<u>You will hear</u>: What does your father do?

<u>You will read</u>: A. He's 50 years old.
                     B. He's a teacher.
                     C. He's hungry.
                     D. He's in Los Angeles.

The best answer to the question "What does your father do?" is B: "He's a teacher." Therefore, you should choose answer B.

16. A. I'm sorry, but I don't know how to do it.
    B. No, it's four blocks in the other direction.
    C. Yes, that's how you say it.
    D. Yes, this used to be Greenview Park.

17. A. I used to go to school there.
    B. It costs two dollars to cross it.
    C. Yes, there is a bridge over there.
    D. The bridge is near the port.

18. A. Careful! Don't break it!
    B. Oh, you don't need to worry about your weight.
    C. I couldn't agree more.
    D. Don't worry. It's my treat.

19. A. No, the line is very long.
    B. No, I just got here.
    C. Yes, I'll wait.
    D. Please don't be too long.

20. A. It was NT$10,000.
    B. It was from London.
    C. At 3:00.
    D. A little bumpy.

21. A. I get two weeks of vacation.
    B. This fall.
    C. Hawaii.
    D. I'd love to.

22. A. No, mine is brown.
    B. No, he's only visiting.
    C. No, he's much taller.
    D. I should get one.

23. A. It opens at 9:00.
    B. It's about a five-minute walk.
    C. I should be there an hour or two.
    D. It doesn't cost anything.

24. A. Yes, I have one.
    B. No, it's too expensive.
    C. Thanks. I like it.
    D. Yes, but it's still running.

25. A. I say it this way.
    B. No, I don't smell anything.
    C. J-O-H-N-S-O-N.
    D. It was my father's.

26. A. I like Halloween.
    B. I usually go to Japan.
    C. I prefer to travel in the summer.
    D. I get a ten-day holiday.

27. A. I came down with a cold.
    B. Yes, I didn't come.
    C. I'd love to go, but I can't.
    D. When is it?

28. A. He's twenty-four this month.
    B. It was built in 1983.
    C. It's ten stories.
    D. They put up new buildings every year.

29. A. At the age of five.
    B. Because we lived near the water.
    C. My father taught me.
    D. At the YMCA.

30. A. No, I don't care.
    B. Is it two for one?
    C. It'll take an hour to make another one.
    D. Thanks, but one piece was enough.

Part C

In Part C, you will hear 15 conversations between a man and a woman. After each conversation, you will hear a question about the conversation. After you hear the question, read the four possible answers in your test book and choose the best answer to the question you have heard.

Example:

<u>You will hear</u>: (Man) How do you go to school every day?

(Woman) Usually by bus. Sometimes by taxi.

Question: How does the woman go to school?

<u>You will read</u>: A. She always goes to school on foot.
B. She usually rides a bike.
C. She takes either a bus or a taxi.
D. She usually goes to school by bus, never by taxi.

The best answer to the question "How does the woman go to school?" is C: "She takes either a bus or a taxi." Therefore, you should choose answer C.

31. A. Daniel.
    B. Their professor.
    C. A stranger.
    D. An extremely tall man.

32. A. At the train station.
    B. Just after ten o'clock.
    C. Within ten minutes.
    D. To Kaohsiung.

33. A. The singer should go
       to jail.
    B. The singer was not
       actually drunk.
    C. The singer should go
       to a special jail.
    D. The singer should be
       given treatment.

34. A. A set.
    B. A pair.
    C. Three.
    D. Four.

35. A. Bored.
    B. Interested.
    C. Happy.
    D. Surprised.

36. A. At least two hundred
       dollars.
    B. The cost of the parts.
    C. No more than $200.
    D. $200 per part.

37. A. That the caller ask for
       more information.
    B. That the caller
       research other tours.
    C. That the caller take
       the less expensive
       tour.
    D. That the caller visit
       the company's
       website.

38. A. He is a professional
       gardener.
    B. He is good at growing
       plants.
    C. He grows only big
       flowers.
    D. He has a secret recipe.

39. A. Running to her office.
    B. Standing behind Miss Clark.
    C. Examining a patient.
    D. Exercising.

40. A. A corner store.
    B. Two blocks away.
    C. A stationery shop.
    D. The station.

41. A. Yes, because he doesn't have to pay.
    B. Yes, because he loves music.
    C. No, because it is at Baker Hall.
    D. No, because he has things to do.

42. A. The boys have promised to win the race.
    B. The first boy will win.
    C. Bill or Greg will win.
    D. Only one person can win.

43. A. He cannot eat snacks in the car.
    B. He wants to save money.
    C. It will take too long.
    D. He does not have enough money.

44. A. The fish is not tasty.
    B. The woman thinks he is silly.
    C. The woman ordered the wrong dish.
    D. He doesn't like his meal.

45. A. To find a map.
    B. On a tour.
    C. Green Park.
    D. A museum.

Listening Test 1 詳解

Part A

For questions number 1 and 2, please look at picture A.

1. (**D**) What is around the corner?

    A. A beggar.

    B. A dog.

    C. A poster.

    D. Garbage.

    * corner (ˈkɔrnɚ) *n.* 角落
    around the corner 在轉角
    beggar (ˈbɛgɚ) *n.* 乞丐
    poster (ˈpostɚ) *n.* 海報
    garbage (ˈgɑrbɪdʒ) *n.* 垃圾

2. (**A**) Please look at picture A again. What does the man look like?

    A. He is dirty.

    B. He would like money.

    C. He is not looking at her.

    D. He likes to smell.

    * *look like* 看起來像⋯
    dirty (ˈdɝtɪ) *adj.* 髒的   like (laɪk) *v.* 喜歡
    look at 看   smell (smɛl) *v.* 聞

For questions number 3 to 5, please look at picture B.

3. (**A**) What is happening?

    A. It is hailing.

    B. They are not happy.

    C. It's a ballgame.

    D. The boy should hurry.

    * happen ('hæpən) v. 發生   hail (hel) v. 下冰雹

    ballgame ('bɔl'gem) n. 球賽   hurry ('hɝɪ) v. 趕快

4. (**A**) Please look at picture B again. Who is running?

    A. The boy and his dog.

    B. Both children.

    C. It's raining very hard.

    D. The umbrella is ruined.

    * hard (hɑrd) adj. 猛烈的

    umbrella (ʌm'brɛlə) n. 雨傘

    ruined ('ruɪnd) adj. 被破壞的

5. (**C**) Please look at picture B again. Where is the dog hurt?

    A. The boy did it.

    B. By the ball.

    C. On the head.

    D. In the eye.

    * hurt (hɝt) v. 使受傷   by (baɪ) prep. 被…

For questions number 6 to 8, please look at picture C.

6. (**C**) What did the old man do?

    A. He prayed.

    B. He gave a compliment.

    C. He fainted.

    D. He caught him.

    * pray〔pre〕v. 祈禱
      compliment〔'kɑmpləmənt〕n. 稱讚
      faint〔fent〕v. 昏倒   catch〔kætʃ〕v. 接住；抓住

7. (**B**) Please look at picture C again. Who are the men?

    A. In front of a statue.

    B. Monks.

    C. Only one is happy.

    D. There are three.

    * *In front of* 在…前面   statue〔'stætʃu〕n. 雕像
      monk〔mʌŋk〕n. 僧侶；和尚

8. (**B**) Please look at picture C again. Where is the statue?

    A. It is beautiful.

    B. On a table.

    C. It is seated.

    D. It is shocking.

    * seated〔'sitɪd〕adj. 坐著的
      shocking〔'ʃɑkɪŋ〕adj. 令人震驚的

For questions number 9 and 10, please look at picture D.

9. (**D**) What is the girl doing?

    A. She is washing her hair.

    B. She is a gardener.

    C. She hears a song.

    D. She is watering a plant.

    * wash〔waʃ〕v. 洗　　hair〔hɛr〕n. 頭髮

      gardener〔'gɑrdṇɚ〕n. 園丁　　hear〔hɪr〕v. 聽見

      song〔sɔŋ〕n. 歌曲　　water〔'wɔtɚ〕v. 給…澆水

      plant〔plænt〕n. 植物

10. (**D**) Please look at picture D again. What is on the table?

    A. It is a kitchen table.

    B. There is a skull.

    C. A girl is at the table.

    D. There is some water.

    * kitchen〔'kɪtʃɪn〕n. 廚房　　skull〔skʌl〕n. 頭蓋骨；頭顱

For questions number 11 to 13, please look at picture E.

11. (**C**) What is in the man's hand?

    A. He has a box.　　B. He hurt his thumb.

    C. It is a hammer.　　D. He is OK.

    * box〔bɑks〕n. 盒子　　thumb〔θʌm〕n. 大姆指

      hammer〔'hæmɚ〕n. 鐵鎚

      OK〔'o'ke〕adj. 好的；沒問題的

12. (**C**) Please look at picture E again. How does the girl feel?

    A. Injured.

    B. OK.

    C. Worried.

    D. Sweaty.

    * feel〔fil〕v. 覺得　　injured〔'ɪndʒəd〕adj. 受傷的
    worried〔'wɜɪd〕adj. 擔心的
    sweaty〔'swɛtɪ〕adj. 汗流浹背的

13. (**B**) Please look at picture E again. What is true?

    A. The man is not hurt.

    B. The man's finger hurts.

    C. The man is happy.

    D. The box is too heavy.

    * finger〔'fɪŋgə〕n. 手指　　hurt〔hɜt〕v. 痛
    heavy〔'hɛvɪ〕adj. 重的

For questions number 14 and 15, please look at picture F.

14. (**C**) What is the problem?

    A. It's some fish.

    B. She is cold.

    C. He cannot start a fire.

    D. The rocks are.

    * problem〔'prɑbləm〕n. 問題　　fish〔fɪʃ〕n. pl. 魚
    cold〔kold〕adj. 冷的　　fire〔faɪr〕n. 火
    start a fire 生火　　rock〔rɑk〕n. 岩石；石頭

15. (**A**) Please look at picture F again. What do they want to eat?

      A. Three fish.   B. Because it is cold.

      C. On the rocks.   D. They are hungry.

     * hungry (ˈhʌŋgrɪ) *adj.* 餓的

Part B

16. (**B**) Is this the way to Greenview Park?

      A. I'm sorry, but I don't know how to do it.

      B. No, it's four blocks in the other direction.

      C. Yes, that's how you say it.

      D. Yes, this used to be Greenview Park.

     * way (we) *n.* 路   block (blɑk) *n.* 街區
     the other 另一個   direction (dəˈrɛkʃən) *n.* 方向
     used to V. 以前…

17. (**A**) Were you ever in Bridgeport?

      A. I used to go to school there.

      B. It costs two dollars to cross it.

      C. Yes, there is a bridge over there.

      D. The bridge is near the port.

     * ever (ˈɛvɚ) *adv.* 曾經   *go to school* 上學
     cost (kɔst) *v.* 需要（錢）   dollar (ˈdɑlɚ) *n.* 元
     cross (krɔs) *v.* 橫越；渡過
     bridge (brɪdʒ) *n.* 橋   *over there* 在那裡
     near (nɪr) *prep.* 在…附近   port (port) *n.* 港口

18. (**C**) This dish of noodles is fantastic!

A. Careful! Don't break it!

B. Oh, you don't need to worry about your weight.

C. I couldn't agree more.

D. Don't worry. It's my treat.

* dish〔dɪʃ〕n. 一盤（的量）
noodle〔'nudl〕n. 麵
fantastic〔fæn'tæstɪk〕adj. 極好的
careful〔'kɛrfəl〕adj. 小心的
break〔brek〕v. 打破　　need〔nid〕v. 需要
worry about 擔心　　weight〔wet〕n. 體重
agree〔ə'gri〕v. 同意
I couldn't agree more. 我非常同意。
treat〔trit〕n. 請客
It's my treat. 我請客。

19. (**B**) Have you been waiting here long?

A. No, the line is very long.

B. No, I just got here.

C. Yes, I'll wait.

D. Please don't be too long.

* wait〔wet〕v. 等
long〔lɔŋ〕adv. 長時間地　adj. 長時間的
line〔laɪn〕n.（等待順序的）行列
I just got here. 我才剛到。

20. (**D**) How was your flight?

    A. It was NT$10,000.

    B. It was from London.

    C. At 3:00.

    D. A little bumpy.

    * flight〔flaɪt〕*n.* 搭飛機旅行

    London〔'lʌndən〕*n.* 倫敦

    a little 有點　　bumpy〔'bʌmpɪ〕*adj.* 顛簸的

21. (**B**) When are you planning to take your vacation?

    A. I get two weeks of vacation.

    B. This fall.

    C. Hawaii.　　　　　　D. I'd love to.

    * plan〔plæn〕*v.* 計劃　　vacation〔ve'keʃən〕*n.* 假期

    take a vacation 休假　　fall〔fɔl〕*n.* 秋天（= *autumn*）

    Hawaii〔hə'waɪ·i〕*n.* 夏威夷　　*I'd love to.* 我很樂意。

22. (**A**) Is this your bag?

    A. No, mine is brown.

    B. No, he's only visiting.

    C. No, he's much taller.

    D. I should get one.

    * bag〔bæg〕*n.* 袋子；包包

    brown〔braʊn〕*adj.* 棕色的

    visit〔'vɪzɪt〕*v.* 拜訪；參觀

    tall〔tɔl〕*adj.* 高的　　get〔gɛt〕*v.* 買

23. (**C**) How long do you plan to spend at the library today?

    A. It opens at 9:00.

    B. It's about a five-minute walk.

    C. I should be there an hour or two.

    D. It doesn't cost anything.

    * *How long~?* ～多久？   spend〔spɛnd〕v. 度過
    library〔'laɪ,brɛrɪ〕n. 圖書館
    open〔'opən〕v. 開放；營業   minute〔'mɪnɪt〕n. 分鐘
    walk〔wɔk〕n. 路程
    a five-minute walk 五分鐘的路程   cost〔kɔst〕v. 花費

24. (**C**) What a gorgeous car you have!

    A. Yes, I have one.

    B. No, it's too expensive.

    C. Thanks. I like it.

    D. Yes, but it's still running.

    * gorgeous〔'gɔrdʒəs〕adj. 極美麗的
    expensive〔ɪk'spɛnsɪv〕adj. 昂貴的
    still〔stɪl〕adv. 仍然   run〔rʌn〕v. 運轉

25. (**C**) Johnson. How do you spell that?

    A. I say it this way.

    B. No, I don't smell anything.

    C. J - O - H - N - S - O - N.

    D. It was my father's.

    * spell〔spɛl〕v. 拼（字）   way〔we〕n. 方式；樣子
    this way 這樣   smell〔smɛl〕v. 聞

26. (**A**) What's your favorite holiday?

    A. I like Halloween.

    B. I usually go to Japan.

    C. I prefer to travel in the summer.

    D. I get a ten-day holiday.

    * favorite〔'fevərɪt〕*adj.* 最喜愛的
      holiday〔'hɑlə‚de〕*n.* 節日;假日
      Halloween〔‚hælo'in〕*n.* 萬聖節前夕(即十月三十一日晚上)
      usually〔'juʒuəlɪ〕*adv.* 通常
      Japan〔dʒə'pæn〕*n.* 日本
      prefer〔prɪ'fɝ〕*v.* 比較喜歡
      travel〔'trævḷ〕*v.* 旅行   summer〔'sʌmɚ〕*n.* 夏天

27. (**A**) Why didn't you come to the party?

    A. I came down with a cold.

    B. Yes, I didn't come.

    C. I'd love to go, but I can't.

    D. When is it?

    * party〔'pɑrtɪ〕*n.* 宴會;派對
      come down with 罹患(疾病)
      cold〔kold〕*n.* 感冒

28. (**B**) How old is this building?

    A. He's twenty-four this month.

    B. It was built in 1983.

C. It's ten stories.

D. They put up new buildings every year.

* building〔'bɪldɪŋ〕*n.* 建築物　　month〔mʌnθ〕*n.* 月
build〔bɪld〕*v.* 建造　　story〔'storɪ〕*n.* 樓層
put up 建造

29. (**A**) When did you learn to swim?

A. At the age of five.

B. Because we lived near the water.

C. My father taught me.

D. At the YMCA.

* learn〔lɜn〕*v.* 學習
swim〔swɪm〕*v.* 游泳　　age〔edʒ〕*n.* 年紀
YMCA 基督教青年會 (= *Young Men's Christian Association*)
【創立於西元 1844 年英國倫敦，而後再逐漸擴展至世界各地。】

30. (**D**) Would you care for more cake?

A. No, I don't care.

B. Is it two for one?

C. It'll take an hour to make another one.

D. Thanks, but one piece was enough.

* *care for* 想要　　more〔mor〕*adj.* 更多的
cake〔kek〕*n.* 蛋糕　　*I don't care.* 我不在乎。
two for one 二合一的　　take〔tek〕*v.* 花費 (時間)
another〔ə'nʌðɚ〕*adj.* 另一個
piece〔pis〕*n.* 片；塊　　enough〔ə'nʌf〕*adj.* 足夠的

Part C

31. (**C**) W: That man looks familiar. Do you know him?

M: No, but he looks a lot like Professor Daniels.

W: You're right, but it's not him.

M: No, Professor Daniels is much taller.

Question : Who are the speakers looking at?

A. Daniel.

B. Their professor.

C. A stranger.

D. An extremely tall man.

* familiar 〔 fə'mɪljə 〕 adj. 熟悉的
  a lot 非常（ = *much* ）　　professor 〔 prə'fɛsə 〕 n. 教授
  right 〔 raɪt 〕 adj. 正確的　　speaker 〔'spikə 〕 n. 說話者
  stranger 〔'strendʒə 〕 n. 陌生人
  extremely 〔 ɪk'strimlɪ 〕 adv. 極度地；非常地

32. (**B**) M: How long must we wait for the train to Kaohsiung?

W: It departs at 10:20, and we can board about five minutes before.

M: OK. So another ten minutes then.

Question : When does this conversation take place?

A. At the train station.

B. Just after ten o'clock.

C. Within ten minutes.

D. To Kaohsiung.

* ***wait for*** 等待　　train〔tren〕*n.* 火車
  Kaohsiung 高雄　　depart〔dɪ'pɑrt〕*v.* 離開；出發
  board〔bord〕*v.* 上（車、船、飛機）
  before〔bɪ'for〕*adv.* 較早地
  another〔ə'nʌðɚ〕*adj.* 另一個
  conversation〔͵kɑnvɚ'seʃən〕*n.* 對話　　***take place*** 發生
  train station 火車站　　within〔wɪð'ɪn〕*prep.* 在…之內

33. (**A**)　W: Have you read the story about the pop singer in today's paper?

　　　M: No. What does it say?

　　　W: She was caught driving drunk last night. Maybe she'll have to go to jail.

　　　M: Well, they shouldn't give her any special treatment.

　　　Question : What does the man imply?

　　　A. The singer should go to jail.

　　　B. The singer was not actually drunk.

　　　C. The singer should go to a special jail.

　　　D. The singer should be given treatment.

* read〔rid〕*v.* 讀；看　　story〔'storɪ〕*n.* (新聞)報導
  pop〔pɑp〕*adj.* 流行的　　singer〔'sɪŋɚ〕*n.* 歌手
  pop singer 流行歌手　　paper〔'pepɚ〕*n.* 報紙
  say〔se〕*v.* (報紙、信等)說　　catch〔kætʃ〕*v.* 逮捕
  drive〔draɪv〕*v.* 駕駛　　drunk〔drʌŋk〕*adj.* 酒醉的
  maybe〔'mebi〕*adv.* 或許　　jail〔dʒel〕*n.* 監獄
  go to jail 坐牢　　special〔'spɛʃəl〕*adj.* 特殊的
  treatment〔'tritmənt〕*n.* 待遇；治療
  imply〔ɪm'plaɪ〕*v.* 暗示
  actually〔'æktʃʊəlɪ〕*adv.* 實際上；真正地

34. (**C**) M : Oh, no! I just broke another glass.

W : Another one? That makes three so far, right?

M : Yes. Maybe I should just go ahead and break the last one.

W : Go ahead. Then you can buy a new set.

Question : How many glasses have been broken?

A. A set.   B. A pair.
C. Three.   D. Four.

* glass〔glæs〕*n.* 玻璃杯   make〔mek〕*v.* 等於
  so far 到目前為止   ***go ahead*** 繼續向前；做吧
  set〔sɛt〕*n.* 一組；一套   pair〔pɛr〕*n.* 一對

35. (**D**) W : Are you watching this?

M : Sort of. It's the final day of the golf tournament.

W : But you don't even like sports!

M : Yeah. But there's nothing else on.

Question : How does the woman feel?

A. Bored.   B. Interested.
C. Happy.   D. Surprised.

* watch〔wɑtʃ〕*v.* 看（電視）   ***sort of*** 有點
  final〔'faɪnl̩〕*adj.* 最後的   golf〔gɑlf〕*n.* 高爾夫球
  tournament〔'tɝnəmənt〕*n.* 錦標賽
  even〔'ivən〕*adv.* 甚至   sport〔sport〕*n.* 運動
  yeah〔jæ〕*adv.* 是的（= *yes*）
  nothing〔'nʌθɪŋ〕*prep.* 沒有什麼（事；東西）

else〔ɛls〕*adj.* 其它的　　on〔ɑn〕*adv.* (電視)播放
bored〔bord〕*adj.* 無聊的
interested〔'ɪntərɪstɪd〕*adj.* 感興趣的
surprised〔sə'praɪzd〕*adj.* 驚訝的

36. (**A**) M : So how much do you think the repairs are going to cost?

W : That depends on whether we have to replace any parts. The labor alone will be about $200.

M : Wow. Am I ever glad I have insurance!

Question : How much will the repairs cost?

A. At least two hundred dollars.

B. The cost of the parts.

C. No more than $200.

D. $200 per part.

* repair〔rɪ'pɛr〕*n.* 修理　　*depend on* 視…而定
whether〔'hwɛðɚ〕*conj.* 是否
replace〔rɪ'ples〕*v.* 更換　　part〔pɑrt〕*n.* 零件
labor〔'lebɚ〕*n.* 勞力　　alone〔ə'lon〕*adv.* 單單；僅僅
wow〔waʊ〕*interj.* 哇；啊
ever〔'ɛvɚ〕*adj.* 曾經　　glad〔glæd〕*adj.* 高興的
insurance〔ɪn'ʃʊrəns〕*n.* 保險
Am I ever glad I have insurance! 我真高興我有保險！
　(= *I'm very glad I have insurance!*)
at least 至少　　cost〔kɔst〕*n.* 費用
no more than 不超過　　per〔pɚ〕*prep.* 每一

37. (**D**) W: Hello. I'm calling about the city tour. Could you give me some information?

M: Actually, there are two tours — a half-day and a full-day. They cost $25 and $40.

W: Can you tell me what sites they cover?

M: Yes, but it might be easier for you to take a look at our website. Full details of the tours are available there. You can also get a discount if you book online.

Question : What does the man suggest?

A. That the caller ask for more information.

B. That the caller research other tours.

C. That the caller take the less expensive tour.

D. That the caller visit the company's website.

* city (ˈsɪtɪ) *n.* 城市   tour (tur) *n.* (短期) 觀光旅行
  I'm calling about the city tour. 我打電話來詢問有關市區
  觀光。(= *I'm calling to ask about the city tour.*)
  information (ˌɪnfɚˈmeʃən) *n.* 資訊
  actually (ˈæktʃʊəlɪ) *adv.* 事實上
  half-day 半天的   ***full-day*** 全天的
  site (saɪt) *n.* 地點   cover (ˈkʌvɚ) *v.* 涵蓋
  take a look at 看一看   website (ˈwɛbˌsaɪt) *n.* 網站
  full (fʊl) *adj.* 完整的   detail (ˈditel) *n.* 細節
  available (əˈveləbl̩) *adj.* 可獲得的
  discount (ˈdɪskaʊnt) *n.* 折扣   book (bʊk) *v.* 預訂
  online (ˈɑnˌlaɪn) *adv.* 在網路上

suggest〔səg'dʒɛst〕v. 建議

caller〔'kɔlɚ〕n. 打電話來的人

ask for 要求　　research〔ri'sɜtʃ〕v. 研究；調查

other〔'ʌðɚ〕adj. 其他的　　take〔tek〕v. 選擇

less〔lɛs〕adv. 較不　　visit〔'vɪzɪt〕v. 參觀；拜訪

company〔'kʌmpənɪ〕n. 公司

38. (**B**) M: How ever did you grow such big, beautiful roses?

W: Oh, I didn't. My husband is the gardener in the
family.

M: Well, I'll have to get his secret. I just can't get my
rose bushes to produce anything!

Question : What is true about the woman's husband?

A. He is a professional gardener.

B. He is good at growing plants.

C. He grows only big flowers.

D. He has a secret recipe.

* **how ever** 究竟是如何　　grow〔gro〕v. 種植

such〔sʌtʃ〕adv. 如此地　　rose〔roz〕n. 玫瑰花

husband〔'hʌzbənd〕n. 丈夫

gardener〔'gɑrdnɚ〕n. 園丁

secret〔'sikrɪt〕n. 秘訣　adj. 秘密的

bush〔buʃ〕n. 灌木叢；矮樹叢

produce〔prə'djus〕v. 生產

professional〔prə'fɛʃn̩l〕adj. 專業的

be good at 擅長　　recipe〔'rɛsəpɪ〕n. 食譜

39. (**C**) W: Good morning. I have an 11:00 appointment with
           Dr. Myer.

       M: Miss Clark? I'm afraid the doctor is running a little
           behind. Please take a seat, and I'll call you when
           she's ready for you.

       W: OK. How long do you think it will be?

       M: About 30 minutes.

       Question : What is the doctor probably doing now?

    A. Running to her office.

    B. Standing behind Miss Clark.

    C. Examining a patient.

    D. Exercising.

    * appointment〔ə'pɔɪntmənt〕n.（診療）約會
      Dr.〔'dɑktɚ〕n. …醫生   Myer〔'maɪɚ〕n. 邁爾
      Clark〔klɑrk〕n. 克拉克
      afraid〔ə'fred〕adj. 恐怕…的
      run〔rʌn〕v.（工作等）進行
      behind〔bɪ'haɪnd〕adv.（工作、進度等）落後
       prep. 在…後面
      take a seat 坐下   call〔kɔl〕v. 叫
      be ready for~ 爲~做好準備
      probably〔'prɑbəblɪ〕adv. 可能
      office〔'ɔfɪs〕n. 辦公室
      examine〔ɪg'zæmɪn〕v. 檢查
      patient〔'peʃənt〕n. 病人
      exercise〔'ɛksɚ,saɪz〕v. 運動

40. (**C**)　M：Do you know where I could pick up some envelopes?

W：There's a stationery store on the corner over there.

M：I tried that, but they're closed today.

W：In that case, there's another one two blocks that way, on your left.

Question：Where does the man want to go?

A. A corner store.　　　B. Two blocks away.

C. A stationery shop.　　D. The station.

* ***pick up*** 買　　envelope (ˈɛnvəˌlop) *n.* 信封
stationery (ˈsteʃənˌɛrɪ) *n.* 文具
stationery store 文具店　　corner (ˈkɔrnə) *n.* 轉角
try (traɪ) *v.* 嘗試　　close (kloz) *v.* 關閉
in that case 那樣的話　　***that way*** 那邊
left (lɛft) *n.* 左邊　　***corner store*** 街角商店
station (ˈsteʃən) *n.* 車站

41. (**A**)　W：Are you interested in the concert at Baker Hall tonight?

M：Not really.　Classical music isn't my thing.

W：Too bad.　I've got some free tickets.

M：Oh!　In that case, I'd love to go.

Question：Does the man want to go to the concert?

A. Yes, because he doesn't have to pay.

B. Yes, because he loves music.

C. No, because it is at Baker Hall.

D. No, because he has things to do.

* **be interested in** 對…有興趣

concert (ˈkɑnsɝt) n. 音樂會

hall (hɔl) n. (音樂、演講會用的) 大廳

not really 不盡然　　classical (ˈklæsɪkḷ) adj. 古典的

music (ˈmjuzɪk) n. 音樂　　thing (θɪŋ) n. 東西；興趣

Too bad. 太可惜了。　　**I've got** 我有

free (fri) adj. 免費的　　ticket (ˈtɪkɪt) n. 入場券

pay (pe) v. 付錢　　love (lʌv) v. 喜愛

42. (**C**) M: Who's the fastest runner in your class?

W: I'm not sure. Either Bill or Greg.

M: I guess we'll find out on Sports Day next week.

W: Yes. One of them is bound to win the race.

Question : What does the woman mean?

A. The boys have promised to win the race.

B. The first boy will win.

C. Bill or Greg will win.

D. Only one person can win.

* runner (ˈrʌnɚ) n. 跑者　　class (klæs) n. 班級

sure (ʃur) adj. 確定的　　**either…or~** 不是…就是~

guess (gɛs) v. 猜　　**find out** 找出 (答案)

next (nɛkst) adj. 下一個的　　**be bound to** 一定會

win (wɪn) v. 贏　　race (res) n. 比賽；賽跑

mean (min) v. 意思是

promise (ˈprɑmɪs) v. 保證；答應

person (ˈpɝsṇ) n. 人

43. (**B**) W: How are we getting to the hot springs?

M: We can take bus number 300. It should be along in ten minutes or so.

W: Why don't we just take a taxi?

M: I'd rather spend my money on snacks.

Question : Why doesn't the man want to take a taxi?

A. He cannot eat snacks in the car.

B. He wants to save money.

C. It will take too long.

D. He does not have enough money.

* *get to* 到達　*hot spring* 溫泉

take〔tek〕*v.* 搭乘（交通工具）

number〔'nʌmbɚ〕*n.* 號碼；第（幾）號

along〔ə'lɔŋ〕*adv.* 過來　*or so* 大約…；…左右

taxi〔'tæksɪ〕*n.* 計程車　*would rather* 寧願

snack〔snæk〕*n.* 零食；點心　save〔sev〕*v.* 節省

44. (**D**) M: Ugh! This is terrible!

W: Really? This restaurant is famous for its seafood chowder.

M: Maybe so, but I don't like fish.

W: Then you shouldn't have ordered it, silly.

Question : Why is the man unhappy?

A. The fish is not tasty.

B. The woman thinks he is silly.

C. The woman ordered the wrong dish.

D. He doesn't like his meal.

* ugh〔ʌg〕*interj.* 啊；哎呀

terrible〔'tɛrəb!〕*adj.* 很糟的　***Really?*** 眞的嗎？

restaurant〔'rɛstərənt〕*n.* 餐廳

famous〔'feməs〕*adj.* 有名的

famous for~ 因~而有名　　seafood〔'si,fud〕*n.* 海鮮

chowder〔'tʃaʊdɚ〕*n.* 濃湯　　so〔so〕*adv.* 如此

order〔'ɔrdɚ〕*v.* 點（餐）

silly〔'sɪlɪ〕*n.* 傻瓜　*adj.* 愚蠢的

unhappy〔ʌn'hæpɪ〕*adj.* 感到不滿的

tasty〔'testɪ〕*adj.* 美味的

wrong〔rɔŋ〕*adj.* 錯誤的　　meal〔mil〕*n.* 餐

45.(**D**)　W: Do you have a map of the area?

M: No, I don't, but I know it's near Green Park.

W: OK.　I'll just ask that man if he knows how to get
　　to the museum or the park.

Question : Where do they want to go?

A. To find a map.

B. On a tour.

C. Green Park.

D. A museum.

* map〔mæp〕*n.* 地圖　　area〔'ɛrɪə〕*n.* 區域

museum〔mju'zɪəm〕*n.* 博物館

find〔faɪnd〕*v.* 找到

English Listening Comprehension Test
Test Book No. 2

This listening comprehension test will test your ability to understand spoken English. In this test, each conversation, statement and question will be spoken JUST ONE TIME. They will not be written out for you. There are three parts to this test. Special instructions will be given to you at the beginning of each part.

Part A

In Part A, you will see several pictures in your test book. For each picture, you will be asked 1 to 3 questions. For each question, you will hear four possible answers. Choose the best answer according to what you see in the picture.

Example:

<u>You will see</u>:

<u>You will hear</u>: What is this?
A. This is a table.
B. This is a chair.
C. This is a watch.
D. This is a doll.

The best answer to the question "What is this?" is B: "This is a chair." Therefore, you should choose answer B.

A. **Questions 1-2**

B. **Questions 3-5**

C. <u>Questions 6-8</u>

D. <u>Questions 9-10</u>

E. Questions 11-13

F. Questions 14-15

Part B

In Part B, you will hear 15 questions. After you hear a question, read the four possible answers in your test book and decide which one is the best answer to the question you have heard.

Example:

You will hear: What does your father do?

You will read: A. He's 50 years old.

B. He's a teacher.

C. He's hungry.

D. He's in Los Angeles.

The best answer to the question "What does your father do?" is B: "He's a teacher." Therefore, you should choose answer B.

16. A. No. Isn't it on the
     table?
   B. I typed it this morning.
   C. I write a paper every
      day.
   D. It's not my paper.

17. A. I like it very much.
   B. I'll have another.
   C. It's too much for me.
   D. Oh, there it is.

18. A. Yes.
    B. Sorry, there are no sales on right now.
    C. Yes, I'll change it for you right away.
    D. It's $200 a night, $250 on weekends.

19. A. Yes, I have.
    B. Madeleine told me about it.
    C. It's a $100 fine.
    D. No, I don't think I can.

20. A. No, but I'll ring you in the morning.
    B. It lasts only half an hour.
    C. Yes, during the summer.
    D. Yes, I do.

21. A. Of course.
    B. Congratulations!
    C. It was a lot of fun.
    D. No, I haven't.

22. A. We could spend two nights at the lake.
    B. How about the salad?
    C. I certainly would.
    D. Let's see a movie.

23. A. I usually go by taxi.
    B. I bought some yesterday.
    C. Just a Coke.
    D. Let's go in a minute.

24. A. Yes, I'd like that.
    B. Once or twice a week.
    C. I like the steak restaurant on First Street.
    D. Yes, it was awful, wasn't it?

25. A. Well, thanks for
       stopping by.
    B. Why don't you go there?
    C. Nice to meet you, too.
    D. It was my pleasure.

26. A. I imagine she can do it.
    B. Good for her.
    C. One more time.
    D. Wait. I'll give you a
       hand.

27. A. I know. He's usually
       late.
    B. Oh. I'm sorry to hear
       that.
    C. Not in a couple of days.
    D. No, I can't hear
       anything.

28. A. Yes, it's occupied.
    B. May I sit down?
    C. I'll take one, too.
    D. No, they're all taken.

29. A. I usually drink tea in
       the morning.
    B. I've seen the movie
       three times.
    C. They're all fine.
    D. I like fishing and
       golf.

30. A. Yes, I made it myself.
    B. No, that's the way
       out.
    C. He said thank you.
    D. It says No Smoking.

Part C

In Part C, you will hear 15 conversations between a man and a woman. After each conversation, you will hear a question about the conversation. After you hear the question, read the four possible answers in your test book and choose the best answer to the question you have heard.

Example:

<u>You will hear</u>: (Man) How do you go to school every day?

(Woman) Usually by bus. Sometimes by taxi.

Question: How does the woman go to school?

<u>You will read</u>: A. She always goes to school on foot.
B. She usually rides a bike.
C. She takes either a bus or a taxi.
D. She usually goes to school by bus, never by taxi.

The best answer to the question "How does the woman go to school?" is C: "She takes either a bus or a taxi." Therefore, you should choose answer C.

31. A. In a classroom.
    B. On an airplane.
    C. On a bus.
    D. In a theater.

32. A. A new flat.
    B. A volunteer.
    C. Assistance.
    D. A real estate agent.

33. A. He has already seen it.
    B. It's not running.
    C. He prefers magazines to dramas.
    D. The TV is missing channel 2.

34. A. Buy the size 8 in black.
    B. Try the size 8 in black.
    C. Try the size 10 in black.
    D. Buy a size 9 in a different color.

35. A. Summer.
    B. A roller coaster.
    C. November.
    D. An amusement park.

36. A. The city is unaware of the problem.
    B. There are not enough parks in the city.
    C. The woman does not like to take her car into town.
    D. The man is ashamed of the city park.

37. A. It is probably very popular.
    B. It is fifteen minutes long.
    C. It starts every five minutes.
    D. You must see it in different theaters.

38. A. Repair the dish.
    B. Heat the dish.
    C. Bring a new dish.
    D. Give the couple a cold dish.

39. A. Find a computer store.
    B. Show off her computer.
    C. Go to the Trade Center.
    D. Get to the bus station.

40. A. He needs more space for his children.
    B. He is buying a house for his kids.
    C. His family is smaller now.
    D. His kids don't visit him anymore.

41. A. Bus tickets to the hospital.
    B. Lucky draw tickets.
    C. Tickets for a medical exam.
    D. Tickets for a charity performance.

42. A. It might be stolen.
    B. It could be towed.
    C. She could get a parking ticket.
    D. The man may drive it away.

43. A. He will not help the woman start the car.
    B. It is not his car.
    C. He cannot see the car.
    D. He did not use the car.

44. A. The building is taking too long to construct.
    B. The woman's building is too old.
    C. The building work is creating a lot of dust.
    D. The construction is making a lot of noise.

45. A. Fried donuts.
    B. A cake.
    C. A pizza.
    D. Soup.

Listening Test 2 詳解

Part A

For questions number 1 and 2, please look at picture A.

1. (**A**) What is in the jar?
   A. It's a bug.   B. It's in his hands.
   C. It's in the water.   D. It's a sink.

   * jar〔dʒɑr〕*n.* 廣口瓶   bug〔bʌg〕*n.* 蟲
     sink〔sɪŋk〕*n.* 水槽

2. (**A**) Please look at picture A again. What might the boy do?
   A. Kill the insect.   B. Take a bath.
   C. He's spilling the water.
   D. He doesn't have to.

   * kill〔kɪl〕*v.* 殺死   insect〔'ɪnsɛkt〕*n.* 昆蟲
     take a bath 洗澡   spill〔spɪl〕*v.* 灑出

For questions number 3 to 5, please look at picture B.

3. (**C**) What happened to the cat?
   A. It cut its hair.   B. It laughed at it.
   C. It was shaven.   D. No, it's not happy.

   * cut〔kʌt〕*v.* 剪   hair〔hɛr〕*n.*（動物的）毛
     laugh〔læf〕*v.* 笑   *laugh at* 嘲笑
     shave〔ʃev〕*v.* 剃毛

4. (**B**) Please look at picture B again. Where is the mouse?

　　A. Because it is funny.　　B. It's in a hole.

　　C. It's his friend.　　D. It has a cough.

　　* mouse〔maʊs〕n. 老鼠　　funny〔'fʌnɪ〕adj. 好笑的

　　　 hole〔hol〕n. 洞　　friend〔frɛnd〕n. 朋友

　　　 cough〔kɔf〕n. 咳嗽　　*have a cough* 咳嗽

5. (**A**) Please look at picture B again. What is the cat looking at?

　　A. Its tail.　　B. It's crying.

　　C. Its feathers.　　D. The mouse is.

　　* tail〔tel〕n. 尾巴　　cry〔kraɪ〕v. 哭

　　　 feather〔'fɛðɚ〕n. 羽毛

For questions number 6 to 8, please look at picture C.

6. (**C**) What is the woman who is wearing a hat?

　　A. She is announcing a sale.

　　B. She is a shopper.

　　C. She is a salesperson.

　　D. She is rich.

　　* wear〔wɛr〕v. 穿著；戴著　　hat〔hæt〕n. 帽子

　　　 announce〔ə'naʊns〕v. 宣布；發表

　　　 sale〔sel〕n. 拍賣　　shopper〔'ʃɑpɚ〕n. 購物者

　　　 salesperson〔'selz,pɝsn̩〕n. 售貨員

　　　 rich〔rɪtʃ〕adj. 有錢的

7. (**B**) Please look at picture C again. What is on the table?

    A. It is on sale.

    B. Women's clothes.

    C. Ten women.

    D. In a department store.

    * table〔'tebḷ〕n. 桌子　　*on sale* 特價；拍賣
    clothes〔kloz〕n. pl. 衣服　　*department store* 百貨公司

8. (**D**) Please look at picture C again. What are the women doing?

    A. Bargaining.

    B. Checking out.

    C. Trying something on.

    D. Grabbing.

    * bargain〔'bɑrgɪn〕v. 討價還價　　*check out* 結帳退房
    try on 試穿　　grab〔græb〕v. 抓住

For questions number 9 and 10, please look at picture D.

9. (**D**) In this picture, where is the girl?

    A. Because she is scared.

    B. She is screaming.

    C. It is a bug.

    D. On the dresser.

    * scared〔skɛrd〕adj. 受驚嚇的
    scream〔skrim〕v. 尖叫
    dresser〔'drɛsɚ〕n.（附有抽屜的）梳妝台

10. (**B**) Please look at picture D again. What will he do?

    A. He is a baseball player.

    B. Kill it.

    C. It's a bat.

    D. He feels upset.

    * baseball〔'bes,bɔl〕n. 棒球　　player〔'pleɚ〕n. 選手
    kill〔kɪl〕v. 殺死　　bat〔bæt〕n. 棒球棒；蝙蝠
    upset〔ʌp'sɛt〕adj. 驚惶失措的；不高興的

For questions number 11 to 13, please look at picture E.

11. (**C**) According to the picture, what did the boy do?

    A. He hurt his ear.

    B. He killed someone.

    C. He broke something.

    D. He is playing.

    * *according to* 根據　　hurt〔hɝt〕v. 弄傷
    ear〔ɪr〕n. 耳朵　　break〔brek〕v. 打破
    play〔ple〕v. 玩耍

12. (**B**) Please look at picture E again. What is on the floor?

    A. It's a window.　　　　B. There is glass.

    C. There are bullets.　　D. It's the first floor.

    * floor〔flor〕n. 地板　　window〔'wɪndo〕n. 窗戶
    glass〔glæs〕n. 玻璃　　bullet〔'bulɪt〕n. 子彈
    the first floor 一樓

13. (**D**) Please look at picture E again. What is the man doing?

    A. He has been hurt.

    B. He is angry.

    C. He is crying.

    D. He is pulling.

    * hurt〔hɜt〕v. 使受傷　　angry〔'æŋgrɪ〕adj. 生氣的
    pull〔pʊl〕v. 拉扯

For questions number 14 and 15, please look at picture F.

14. (**A**) What does the boy have on?

    A. A cape.

    B. A sidewalk.

    C. A gift.

    D. A prize.

    * *have on* 穿著；戴著　　cape〔kep〕n. 披風
    sidewalk〔'saɪd,wɔk〕n. 人行道
    gift〔gɪft〕n. 禮物　　prize〔praɪz〕n. 獎品

15. (**C**) Please look at picture F again. What day is this?

    A. Her birthday.

    B. It is evening.

    C. Halloween.

    D. The first.

    * birthday〔'bɝθ,de〕n. 生日
    Halloween〔,hælo'in〕n. 萬聖節前夕（即十月三十一日晚上）
    first〔fɝst〕n.（每月的）一號

Part B

16. (**A**) Have you seen today's paper?

    A. No. Isn't it on the table?

    B. I typed it this morning.

    C. I write a paper every day.

    D. It's not my paper.

    * paper〔'pepɚ〕n. 報紙 (= *newspaper*)；報告
      type〔taɪp〕v. 打字

17. (**C**) Can't you finish your burger?

    A. I like it very much.

    B. I'll have another.

    C. It's too much for me.

    D. Oh, there it is.

    * finish〔'fɪnɪʃ〕v. 吃完
      burger〔'bɝgɚ〕n. 漢堡 (= *hamburger*)
      another〔ə'nʌðɚ〕*pron.* 另一個
      be too much for *sb*. 對某人而言太多了
      there it is 這就在那裡

18. (**D**) Could you tell me how much you charge for a double room?

    A. Yes.

    B. Sorry, there are no sales on right now.

    C. Yes, I'll change it for you right away.

    D. It's $200 a night, $250 on weekends.

* charge〔tʃɑrdʒ〕v. 收費　　double〔'dʌbḷ〕adj. 兩人用的
  double room 雙人房　　sale〔sel〕n. 特價；拍賣
  on〔ɑn〕adv. 舉行中；進行中　　**right now** 現在
  change〔tʃendʒ〕v. 改變；更換
  right away 馬上；立刻　　weekend〔'wik'ɛnd〕n. 週末

19. (**B**) How ever did you find this place?

　　A. Yes, I have.

　　B. Madeleine told me about it.

　　C. It's a $100 fine.

　　D. No, I don't think I can.

　　* **how ever** 究竟是如何　　find〔faɪnd〕v. 找到
　　place〔ples〕n. 地方
　　Madeleine〔'mædəlɪn〕n. 瑪德琳
　　tell sb. **about** sth. 告訴某人關於某事
　　fine〔faɪn〕n. 罰款

20. (**C**) Does it often rain in the afternoon?

　　A. No, but I'll ring you in the morning.

　　B. It lasts only half an hour.

　　C. Yes, during the summer.

　　D. Yes, I do.

　　* often〔'ɔfən〕adv. 常常　　rain〔ren〕v. 下雨
　　ring〔rɪŋ〕v. 打電話給
　　last〔læst〕v. 持續　　half〔hæf〕adj. 一半的
　　hour〔aʊr〕n. 小時　　during〔'dʊrɪŋ〕prep. 在…期間
　　summer〔'sʌmɚ〕n. 夏天

21. (**A**) Will you come to Johnny's graduation party?
    A. Of course.   B. Congratulations!
    C. It was a lot of fun.   D. No, I haven't.

    * graduation〔͵grædʒʊˈeʃən〕*n.* 畢業   *Of course.* 當然。
      congratulations〔kən͵grætʃəˈleʃənz〕*n. pl.* 恭喜
      a lot of 許多   fun〔fʌn〕*n.* 樂趣

22. (**D**) What would you like to do tonight?
    A. We could spend two nights at the lake.
    B. How about the salad?
    C. I certainly would.
    D. Let's see a movie.

    * *would like* 想要   spend〔spɛnd〕*v.* 度過
      lake〔lek〕*n.* 湖   *How about~?* ~如何？
      salad〔ˈsæləd〕*n.* 沙拉
      certainly〔ˈsɝtn̩lɪ〕*adv.* 當然；一定
      movie〔ˈmuvɪ〕*n.* 電影

23. (**C**) Can I bring you anything from the store?
    A. I usually go by taxi.
    B. I bought some yesterday.
    C. Just a Coke.
    D. Let's go in a minute.

    * bring〔brɪŋ〕*v.* 帶（東西）給   store〔stor〕*n.* 商店
      usually〔ˈjuʒʊəlɪ〕*adv.* 通常
      by〔baɪ〕*prep.* 搭乘（交通工具）   taxi〔ˈtæksɪ〕*n.* 計程車
      Coke〔kok〕*n.* 可口可樂   *in a minute* 立刻

24. (**B**) How often do you like to eat out?

    A. Yes, I'd like that.

    B. Once or twice a week.

    C. I like the steak restaurant on First Street.

    D. Yes, it was awful, wasn't it?

    * **eat out** 在外面吃飯   once〔wʌns〕*adv.* 一次
    twice〔twaɪs〕*adv.* 兩次   steak〔stek〕*n.* 牛排
    street〔strit〕*n.* 街   awful〔'ɔfʊl〕*adj.* 很糟的

25. (**A**) I really have to be going now.

    A. Well, thanks for stopping by.

    B. Why don't you go there?

    C. Nice to meet you, too.

    D. It was my pleasure.

    * really〔'rɪəlɪ〕*adv.* (加強語氣) 眞的   **have to** 必須
    stop by 順道拜訪   nice〔naɪs〕*adj.* 好的
    meet〔mit〕*v.* 認識   **Nice to meet you.** 很高興認識你。
    pleasure〔'plɛʒɚ〕*n.* 榮幸

26. (**B**) Did you hear? Janet won the singing competition!

    A. I imagine she can do it.

    B. Good for her.

    C. One more time.

    D. Wait. I'll give you a hand.

    * hear〔hɪr〕*v.* 聽到 (消息)   Janet〔'dʒænɪt〕*n.* 珍妮特
    singing〔'sɪŋɪŋ〕*n.* 唱歌
    competition〔͵kɑmpə'tɪʃən〕*n.* 比賽

imagine〔ɪ'mædʒɪn〕v. 想像
Good for her. 做的好；真棒。
one more time 再一次　　wait〔wet〕v. 等
give sb. a hand 幫助某人

27.(**C**) Have you heard from Pete lately?

　　A. I know.　He's usually late.

　　B. Oh.　I'm sorry to hear that.

　　C. Not in a couple of days.

　　D. No, I can't hear anything.

　　* ***hear from*** 得到～的消息　　lately〔'letlɪ〕adv. 最近
　　late〔let〕adj. 遲到的　　sorry〔'sɔrɪ〕adj. 難過的
　　a couple of 兩個；幾個　　hear〔hɪr〕v. 聽到

28.(**D**) There aren't any more seats, are there?

　　A. Yes, it's occupied.　　B. May I sit down?

　　C. I'll take one, too.　　D. No, they're all taken.

　　* seat〔sit〕n. 座位　　occupied〔'ɑkjə,paɪd〕adj. 被佔據的
　　take〔tek〕v. 佔（位子）

29.(**D**) Tell me about your hobbies.

　　A. I usually drink tea in the morning.

　　B. I've seen the movie three times.

　　C. They're all fine.

　　D. I like fishing and golf.

　　* hobby〔'hɑbɪ〕n. 嗜好　　tea〔ti〕n. 茶
　　time〔taɪm〕n. 次數　　fine〔faɪn〕adj. 好的
　　fishing〔'fɪʃɪŋ〕n. 釣魚　　golf〔gɑlf〕n. 高爾夫球

30. (**D**)　Can you make out that sign?

　　A. Yes, I made it myself.

　　B. No, that's the way out.

　　C. He said thank you.

　　D. It says No Smoking.

　　* ***make out*** 辨認出；看出　　sign〔saɪn〕*n.* 告示；標誌

　　　make〔mek〕*v.* 做；製造　　way〔we〕*n.* 方向

　　　out〔aʊt〕*adv.* 出去　　smoke〔smok〕*v.* 抽煙

　　　No Smoking 禁止吸煙

Part C

31. (**D**)　W: Excuse me, but you're in my seat.

　　M: I am?　But my ticket is for Row T, Seat 12.

　　W: This is row S, not row T.

　　M: Oh.　I'm so sorry.

　　Question : Where are they?

　　A. In a classroom.　　　B. On an airplane.

　　C. On a bus.　　　　　D. In a theater.

　　* ticket〔'tɪkɪt〕*n.* 票　　row〔ro〕*n.* 排

　　　classroom〔'klæs,rum〕*n.* 教室

　　　airplane〔'ɛr,plen〕*n.* 飛機　　theater〔'θiətɚ〕*n.* 戲院

32. (**C**)　M: Oh, no.　We have a flat.

　　W: Well, we'd better change it.　We're not going
　　　　anywhere until we do.

　　M: Are you volunteering?

　　W: Not on your life.　Let's call someone.

Question : What do they need?

A. A new flat.　　　　B. A volunteer.

C. Assistance.　　　　D. A real estate agent.

* flat〔flæt〕 *n.* 洩了氣的輪胎（= *flat tire*）；公寓

  had better V. 最好～　　change〔tʃendʒ〕 *v.* 更換

  anywhere〔'ɛnɪˌhwɛr〕 *adv.* 任何地方

  not… until～　直到～才…

  volunteer〔ˌvɑlən'tɪr〕 *v.* 自願　　*n.* 自願者

  Not on your life. 你休想。

  assistance〔ə'sɪstəns〕 *n.* 幫助　　estate〔ə'stet〕 *n.* 地產

  real estate 不動產　　agent〔'edʒənt〕 *n.* 經紀人；代理人

33. (**A**)　W: Let's watch the drama on channel 2.

　　　　　　M: But it's a rerun.

　　　　　　W: It is?　Then it's one I missed.

　　　　　　M: You go ahead then.　I'll just read my magazine.

　　Question : Why won't the man watch the drama?

　　A. He has already seen it.

　　B. It's not running.

　　C. He prefers magazines to dramas.

　　D. The TV is missing channel 2.

* drama〔'drɑmə〕 *n.* 戲劇　　channel〔'tʃænl̩〕 *n.* 頻道

  rerun〔ri'rʌn〕 *n.* 重播　　miss〔mɪs〕 *v.* 錯過；缺少

  go ahead 你請便；做吧

  magazine〔ˌmægə'zin〕 *n.* 雜誌

  already〔ɔl'rɛdɪ〕 *adv.* 已經

  prefer A *to* B　喜歡 A 甚於 B

34. (**C**) M: The size 8 is a little tight. Do you have a size 9?

W: The jacket comes in even sizes only. Do you want to try the next size up?

M: Sure, if you've got it in black.

Question : What will the man do?

A. Buy the size 8 in black.

B. Try the size 8 in black.

C. Try the size 10 in black.

D. Buy a size 9 in a different color.

* size〔saɪz〕*n.* 尺寸　　*a little* 有點

tight〔taɪt〕*adj.* 緊的　　jacket〔'dʒækɪt〕*n.* 夾克

come in 有…（尺寸、顏色、形狀等）

even〔'ivən〕*adj.* 偶數的　　*the next* 下一個

the next size up 大一個尺寸　　*Sure.* 當然。

have got 有　　black〔blæk〕*n.* 黑色

different〔'dɪfrənt〕*adj.* 不同的

color〔'kʌlɚ〕*n.* 顏色

35. (**C**) W: I'm surprised there aren't more people here today.

M: Well, this is the slow season. You should see this place during the summer holiday.

W: I bet. We'd probably have to wait an hour for every ride.

M: Yep, you're lucky. You can get on the roller coaster in five minutes today.

Question : When does this conversation take place?

A. Summer.　　　　　B. A roller coaster.

C. November.　　　　D. An amusement park.

* surprised〔sə'praɪzd〕adj. 驚訝的
  slow〔slo〕adj. 不景氣的
  season〔'sizn̩〕n. 季節；時期
  slow season 淡季　　place〔ples〕n. 地方
  during〔'dʊrɪŋ〕prep. 在…期間
  holiday〔'hɑlə,de〕n. 節日；假日
  the summer holiday 暑假　　bet〔bɛt〕v. 打賭
  I bet. 的確。　　probably〔'prɑbəblɪ〕adv. 可能
  ride〔raɪd〕n.（遊樂場等的）乘坐物
  yep〔jɛp〕adv. 是的【口語 yes】
  lucky〔'lʌkɪ〕adj. 幸運的　　**get on** 坐上
  roller coaster 雲霄飛車　　**take place** 發生
  November〔no'vɛmbɚ〕n. 十一月
  amusement〔ə'mjuzmənt〕n. 娛樂；樂趣
  amusement park 遊樂場

36. (**C**) M: Do you often drive into town?

W: Hardly ever. It's too hard to park.

M: That's a shame. The city should provide more parking.

W: Well, they've been talking about it.

Question: What is true?

A. The city is unaware of the problem.

B. There are not enough parks in the city.

C. The woman does not like to take her car into town.

D. The man is ashamed of the city park.

* drive〔draɪv〕v. 開車　　town〔taun〕n. 城鎮；市區
  hardly〔'hɑrdlɪ〕adv. 幾乎不　　*hardly ever* 非常少
  hard〔hɑrd〕adj. 困難的
  park〔pɑrk〕v. 停車　n. 公園
  too…to~ 太…以致於不能~
  shame〔ʃem〕n. 遺憾的事　　city〔'sɪtɪ〕n. 城市
  provide〔prə'vaɪd〕v. 提供
  parking〔'pɑrkɪŋ〕n. 停車處　　*talk about* 談論
  unaware〔͵ʌnə'wɛr〕adj. 未覺察的；不知道的＜*of*＞
  problem〔'prɑbləm〕n. 問題　　take〔tek〕v. 搭乘
  ashamed〔ə'ʃemd〕adj. 感到羞愧的＜*of*＞

37. (**A**)　W：When is the next showing of Death Aliens IV?

　　　　　M：It starts in five minutes.

　　　　　W：Huh? The last one started just ten minutes ago!

　　　　　M：We have it playing in more than one theater.

　　　　　Question：What is true about the movie?

　　　　　A. It is probably very popular.

　　　　　B. It is fifteen minutes long.

　　　　　C. It starts every five minutes.

　　　　　D. You must see it in different theaters.

* showing〔'ʃoɪŋ〕n. (電影的) 上映
  death〔dɛθ〕n. 死亡　　alien〔'eljən〕n. 外星人
  IV 第四【唸成 the fourth】　　huh〔hʌ〕interj. 哈；什麼？
  last〔læst〕adj. 最後的　　play〔ple〕v. 播放
  more than 超過；不只
  popular〔'pɑpjələ〕adj. 受歡迎的

38. (**C**) M: Excuse me, but this dish is cold.

   W: Oh. I'm so sorry. I'll replace it right away.

   M: How long will that take?

   W: Just a couple of minutes, sir.

   Question : What will the woman do?

   A. Repair the dish.

   B. Heat the dish.

   C. Bring a new dish.

   D. Give the couple a cold dish.

   * dish〔dɪʃ〕 n. 菜餚   replace〔rɪ'ples〕 v. 更換
   right away 立刻   take〔tek〕 v. 花費 (時間)
   a couple of 幾個   repair〔rɪ'pɛr〕 n. 修理
   heat〔hit〕 v. 使…變熱   couple〔'kʌpl̩〕 n. 一對男女

39. (**C**) W: I wonder if you could tell me how to get to the
       Trade Center.

   M: Sure. Just take bus 500 from the corner there. It's
       the last stop. What's going on there today?

   W: There's a big computer show.

   M: Really? Maybe I should come along with you.

   Question : What does the woman want to do?

   A. Find a computer store.

   B. Show off her computer.

   C. Go to the Trade Center.

   D. Get to the bus station.

* wonder〔'wʌndɚ〕*v.* 想知道

　if〔ɪf〕*conj.* 是否　　***get to*** 到達

　trade〔tred〕*n.* 貿易　　center〔'sɛntɚ〕*n.* 中心

　corner〔'kɔrnɚ〕*n.* 轉角　　stop〔stɑp〕*n.* 停車站

　go on 發生；進行　　computer〔kəm'pjutɚ〕*n.* 電腦

　show〔ʃo〕*n.* 展示會　　***computer show*** 電腦展

　come along with *sb.* 跟某人一起去　　***show off*** 炫耀

40.(**C**)　M：Do you know anyone in real estate?

　　　　W：Hm. There's Judy Smith. She's an agent. Why?

　　　　M：I've decided to sell my house and move to a
　　　　　　smaller place.

　　　　W：I guess you don't need all that space now that your
　　　　　　kids are gone.

　　　　Question：Why is the man selling his house?

　　　　A. He needs more space for his children.

　　　　B. He is buying a house for his kids.

　　　　C. His family is smaller now.

　　　　D. His kids don't visit him anymore.

* ***real estate*** 不動產　　Hm〔həm〕*interj.* 嗯；哦（= *hum*）

　agent〔'edʒənt〕*n.* 經紀人；代理人

　decide〔dɪ'saɪd〕*v.* 決定　　sell〔sɛl〕*v.* 賣

　move〔muv〕*v.* 搬家　　place〔ples〕*n.* 地方；住處

　guess〔gɛs〕*v.* 猜　　space〔spes〕*n.* 空間

　now that 既然　　kid〔kɪd〕*n.* 小孩

　gone〔gɔn〕*adj.* 離去的　　family〔'fæməlɪ〕*n.* 家庭

　visit〔'vɪzɪt〕*v.* 拜訪　　***not⋯anymore*** 不再⋯

41. (**D**)　W: So how many tickets did you sell?

M: More than 300!

W: That's terrific.　The money will go a long way toward paying for the hospital's new roof.

M: And I'm really happy that we'll have such a big audience for the benefit concert.

Question : What kind of tickets are they selling?

A. Bus tickets to the hospital.

B. Lucky draw tickets.

C. Tickets for a medical exam.

D. Tickets for a charity performance.

* terrific〔təˋrɪfɪk〕*adj.* 極好的

toward〔təˋword〕*prep.* 對於

go a long way toward … 對…大有用處

pay for 支付…的錢　　hospital〔ˋhɑspɪtl〕*n.* 醫院

roof〔ruf〕*n.* 屋頂　　audience〔ˋɔdɪəns〕*n.* 觀眾

benefit〔ˋbɛnəfɪt〕*n.* 義演　　***benefit concert*** 慈善音樂會

kind〔kaɪnd〕*n.* 種類　　***lucky draw ticket*** 抽獎券

medical〔ˋmɛdɪkl〕*adj.* 醫療的　　exam〔ɪgˋzæm〕*n.* 檢查

charity〔ˋtʃærətɪ〕*n.* 慈善機構

performance〔pɚˋfɔrməns〕*n.* 表演

42. (**B**)　M: Is that your car on the corner?

W: Yes, it is.　Why?

M: You parked in a tow away zone.　If you leave it there, it might be gone when you get back.

W: I didn't know.　Thanks for telling me.

Question : What might happen to the woman's car?

A. It might be stolen.　　　B. It could be towed.

C. She could get a parking ticket.

D. The man may drive it away.

* park〔park〕v. 停車　　tow〔to〕v. 拖
zone〔zon〕n. 區域　　**tow away zone** 拖吊區
leave〔liv〕v. 留下　　gone〔gɔn〕adj. 消失的
happen〔'hæpən〕v. 發生　　steal〔stil〕v. 偷
parking ticket 違規停車罰單　　**drive～away** 把～開走

43.(**D**) W: Did you use the car last night?

M: No.　Why?

W: Someone left the headlights on and now it won't start.

M: Well, don't look at me!

Question : What does the man mean?

A. He will not help the woman start the car.

B. It is not his car.

C. He cannot see the car.

D. He did not use the car.

* headlight〔'hɛd,laɪt〕n.（汽車的）前燈；大燈
on〔an〕adj. 開著的　　start〔stɑrt〕v. 發動

44.(**D**) M: What's making all that racket?

W: They're putting up a new building next door.

M: That's terrible.　How long have you had to put up
with it?

Question : What is the problem?

A. The building is taking too long to construct.

B. The woman's building is too old.

C. The building work is creating a lot of dust.

D. The construction is making a lot of noise.

* racket (ˊrækɪt) n. 喧嘩；吵鬧
  make a racket 發出吵鬧聲　　*put up* 建造
  building (ˊbɪldɪŋ) n. 建築物　　door (dor) n. 門；戶
  next door 隔壁　　terrible (ˊtɛrəbl̩) adj. 很糟的
  put up with 忍受　　construct (kənˊstrʌkt) v. 建造
  create (krɪˊet) v. 產生　　dust (dʌst) n. 灰塵
  construction (kənˊstrʌkʃən) n. 建築工程
  noise (nɔɪz) n. 噪音

45. (**B**) W: What temperature should I set the oven for?

M: 350 degrees, but wait. I'm not sure we have all the ingredients we need.

W: What are we missing?

M: I can't find the eggs or sugar.

Question : What are they making?

A. Fried donuts.　　　　B. A cake.

C. A pizza.　　　　　　D. Soup.

* temperature (ˊtɛmprətʃɚ) n. 溫度　　set (sɛt) v. 設定
  oven (ˊʌvən) n. 烤箱　　degree (dɪˊgri) n. 度
  ingredient (ɪnˊgridɪənt) n. 材料　　miss (mɪs) v. 遺漏
  egg (ɛg) n. 雞蛋　　sugar (ˊʃugɚ) n. 糖
  fried (fraɪd) adj. 油炸的　　donut (ˊdo͵nʌt) n. 甜甜圈
  pizza (ˊpitsə) n. 披薩　　soup (sup) n. 湯

English Listening Comprehension Test
Test Book No. 3

This listening comprehension test will test your ability to understand spoken English. In this test, each conversation, statement and question will be spoken JUST ONE TIME. They will not be written out for you. There are three parts to this test. Special instructions will be given to you at the beginning of each part.

Part A

In Part A, you will see several pictures in your test book. For each picture, you will be asked 1 to 3 questions. For each question, you will hear four possible answers. Choose the best answer according to what you see in the picture.

Example:

<u>You will see</u>:

<u>You will hear</u>: What is this?
    A. This is a table.
    B. This is a chair.
    C. This is a watch.
    D. This is a doll.

The best answer to the question "What is this?" is B: "This is a chair." Therefore, you should choose answer B.

A. <u>Questions 1-3</u>

B. <u>Questions 4-6</u>

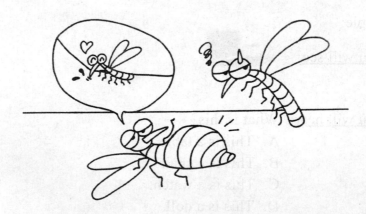

C. <u>Questions 7-8</u>

D. <u>Questions 9-11</u>

E. Questions 12-13

F. Questions 14-15

Part B

In Part B, you will hear 15 questions. After you hear a question, read the four possible answers in your test book and decide which one is the best answer to the question you have heard.

Example:

<u>You will hear</u>: What does your father do?

<u>You will read</u>: A. He's 50 years old.

B. He's a teacher.

C. He's hungry.

D. He's in Los Angeles.

The best answer to the question "What does your father do?" is B: "He's a teacher." Therefore, you should choose answer B.

16. A. Thank you, but it's nothing.

B. I'll have that, too.

C. It's lasagna.

D. It's Tuesday.

17. A. Here it is.

B. How much is it?

C. No, I don't know when I bought it.

D. Yes, I remember him.

18. A. It was in the mailbox.
    B. What's the address?
    C. Try the stationery store.
    D. That'll be 85 cents.

19. A. Some ketchup, please.
    B. No, that's all.
    C. I'd like to have it well-done.
    D. With cream and sugar.

20. A. When I was eighteen.
    B. No, my sister is.
    C. I'm 180 centimeters.
    D. In Taipei.

21. A. I started here two months ago.
    B. It's a vacuum cleaner.
    C. It's Phil's.
    D. Turn the key first.

22. A. Yes, she is.
    B. No, she's my friend.
    C. Yes, Mary and Rachel are friends.
    D. Of course you are.

23. A. I'll put it on my calendar.
    B. That sounds good.
    C. I'll probably see a movie.
    D. Yes, I have to do it.

24. A. From Taiwan University.
    B. I'm an English major.
    C. Last year.
    D. Yes, I'll go to graduate school.

25. A. Yes, when I was a kid.

    B. Yes, I used it.

    C. I put back in the box.

    D. Sure, let's do it.

26. A. Yes, I just finished it.

    B. No, it's due
       tomorrow.

    C. We had to read
       Chapter Four.

    D. I'm sure she'll assign
       something.

27. A. Sure, I can do it.

    B. Watching television.

    C. I do the housework.

    D. I'll answer it in a
       minute.

28. A. I'll have the chicken.

    B. Thanks. That was quick.

    C. Yes, you may.

    D. No, I'm the younger
       one.

29. A. Sorry, but I don't have
       time right now.

    B. It costs NT$30 per hour.

    C. I spend around 300 a
       week.

    D. About two hours a day.

30. A. Nice to meet you, too.

    B. He's a salesman.

    C. Fine, thank you.

    D. He does a very good
       job.

Part C

In Part C, you will hear 15 conversations between a man and a woman. After each conversation, you will hear a question about the conversation. After you hear the question, read the four possible answers in your test book and choose the best answer to the question you have heard.

Example:

<u>You will hear</u>: (Man)   How do you go to school every day?

(Woman) Usually by bus. Sometimes by taxi.

Question: How does the woman go to school?

<u>You will read</u>: A. She always goes to school on foot.
B. She usually rides a bike.
C. She takes either a bus or a taxi.
D. She usually goes to school by bus, never by taxi.

The best answer to the question "How does the woman go to school?" is C: "She takes either a bus or a taxi." Therefore, you should choose answer C.

31. A. The woman is not capable of carrying the sofa.
    B. They have a limited amount of money.
    C. Their friend Buddy will give them some furniture.
    D. They only need to move the furniture, not replace it.

32. A. The man lives further away than the woman.
    B. The woman lives five miles from her office.
    C. The woman took the highway back to her home.
    D. Both the man and the woman drive to work.

33. A. She would have saved money if she had bought the stereo later.
    B. She should have waited for the man to buy the stereo.
    C. She spent NT$12,000 too much for the stereo.
    D. The man should calm down before he buys a stereo.

34. A. The woman asked him to.
    B. He has a virus.
    C. It may be causing his cough.
    D. He doesn't allow smoking in the office.

35. A. She doesn't like coffee.
    B. She does not need to know about the project.
    C. The coffee is very good.
    D. She does not expect the man to pay for her.

36. A. Scary.
    B. Superstitious.
    C. Scarred.
    D. Suspicious.

37. A. He does not like boats.
    B. He has the flu.
    C. He is not in a hurry.
    D. The bridge is too far.

38. A. No one else is
    swimming there.
    B. They thinks it's not
    safe enough.
    C. It's not allowed.
    D. They saw someone
    guarding the beach.

39. A. Spicy.
    B. Cool and snowy.
    C. Freezing temperatures.
    D. Hot and dry.

40. A. She cannot read.
    B. She forgot to write
    something down.
    C. She has bad
    handwriting.
    D. She is nearsighted.

41. A. A dinner party.
    B. A meeting.
    C. A housewarming
    party.
    D. A furniture sale.

42. A. Postage is too expensive.
    B. They will arrive before
    Christmas.
    C. It was faster to write
    them.
    D. He has more time this
    Christmas.

43. A. At the coffee shop.
    B. At three o'clock.
    C. Tomorrow morning.
    D. 2:45 p.m.

44. A. Yes, because he is
    turning left.
    B. No, because he will get
    a ticket.
    C. Yes, because children
    are not in school.
    D. No, because it is 6 p.m.

45. A. It is dangerous.
    B. It is falling down.
    C. It is being moved.
    D. It is being cut down.

Listening Test 3 詳解

Part A

For questions number 1 to 3, please look at picture A.

1. (**C**) Where is the man?

    A. Tired.

    B. On the blanket.

    C. In bed.

    D. A sleepwalker.

    * tired〔taɪrd〕*adj.* 疲倦的

      blanket〔'blæŋkɪt〕*n.* 毛毯

      bed〔bɛd〕*n.* 床

      sleepwalker〔'slip,wɔkɚ〕*n.* 夢遊者

2. (**C**) Please look at picture A again. What time is it?

    A. It is breakfast time.

    B. It is time to go to bed.

    C. It is the middle of the night.

    D. It is midnight.

    * ***It's time to*** ~ 該是~的時候了

      go to bed 上床睡覺

      middle〔'mɪdl̩〕*n.* 中間

      the middle of the night 半夜

      midnight〔'mɪd,naɪt〕*n.* 午夜（即晚上 12:00）

3. (**B**) Please look at picture A again. What happened?

    A. The man wants to sleep.

    B. An insect got in the room.

    C. The man hurt himself.

    D. The alarm went off.

    * happen (ˈhæpən) v. 發生   sleep (slip) v. 睡覺
      insect (ˈɪnsɛkt) n. 昆蟲   ***get in*** 進入
      hurt (hɜt) v. 弄傷   alarm (əˈlɑrm) n. 鬧鐘
      go off (鬧鐘) 響

For questions number 4 to 6, please look at picture B.

4. (**A**) How many insects are there?

    A. There are two.

    B. There are three.

    C. They are mosquitoes.

    D. They are different.

    * mosquito (məˈskito) n. 蚊
      different (ˈdɪfrənt) adj. 不同的

5. (**B**) Please look at picture B again. What is the one on the left doing?

    A. Biting someone.   B. Telling a story.

    C. It is fat.   D. It cannot fly.

    * left (lɛft) n. 左邊   bite (baɪt) v. 咬
      tell a story 說故事   fat (fæt) adj. 胖的
      fly (flaɪ) v. 飛

6. (**A**) Please look at picture B again. How many wings does each insect have?

    A. Two.   B. Three.

    C. Six.   D. Nine.

    * wing〔wɪŋ〕n. 翅膀

For questions number 7 and 8, please look at picture C.

7. (**C**) What happened to the girl?

    A. Because it is a bear.   B. In the park.

    C. She fainted.   D. She loves him.

    * bear〔bɛr〕n. 熊   faint〔fent〕v. 昏倒

8. (**B**) Please look at picture C again. What is the boy holding?

    A. A bear.   B. A mask.

    C. A gift.   D. A girl.

    * hold〔hold〕v. 握；拿   mask〔mæsk〕n. 面具
    gift〔gɪft〕n. 禮物

For questions number 9 to 11, please look at picture D.

9. (**A**) What is in the pan?

    A. A crab.   B. A fire.

    C. Some sauce.   D. The stove.

    * pan〔pæn〕n. 平底鍋   crab〔kræb〕n. 螃蟹
    fire〔faɪr〕n. 火   sauce〔sɔs〕n. 醬；調味汁
    stove〔stov〕n. 爐子

10. (**B**) Please look at picture D again. What is in her hand?

    A. Her mouth.   B. A bottle.

    C. It is hot.   D. On her face.

    * mouth〔mauθ〕 *n.* 嘴巴
       bottle〔'batl̩〕 *n.* 瓶子

11. (**B**) Please look at picture D again. What is the girl trying to do?

    A. Feed her pet.

    B. Cook her lunch.

    C. Some seafood.

    D. She is playing a game.

    * try〔traɪ〕 *v.* 試圖   feed〔fid〕 *v.* 餵
       pet〔pɛt〕 *n.* 寵物   cook〔kʊk〕 *v.* 煮
       seafood〔'si,fud〕 *n.* 海鮮   ***play a game*** 玩遊戲

For questions number 12 and 13, please look at picture E.

12. (**D**) What is on his lap?

    A. A devil is on his left.

    B. A noise.

    C. Nothing.

    D. A newspaper.

    * lap〔læp〕 *n.* 膝部   devil〔'dɛvl̩〕 *n.* 惡魔
       noise〔nɔɪz〕 *n.* 噪音
       newspaper〔'njuz,pepɚ〕 *n.* 報紙

13. (**B**) Please look at picture E again. What is the boy doing?

    A. Getting angry.

    B. Ignoring her.

    C. Shouting.

    D. Listening carefully.

    * angry〔'æŋgrɪ〕*adj.* 生氣的

      ignore〔ɪg'nor〕*v.* 忽視

      shout〔ʃaʊt〕*v.* 大叫   listen〔'lɪsn̩〕*v.* 聽

      carefully〔'kɛrfəlɪ〕*adv.* 小心地；仔細地

For questions number 14 and 15, please look at picture F.

14. (**B**) What can the boy do?

    A. He is sleeping.

    B. Stand on his hands.

    C. Upside down.

    D. Be a clown.

    * ***stand on*** 用…站立   ***upside down*** 上下顛倒

      clown〔klaʊn〕*n.* 小丑

15. (**D**) Please look at picture F again. What is in the bowl?

    A. A table.   B. A wall.

    C. A question mark.

    D. A fish.

    * bowl〔bol〕*n.* 碗；碗狀物   wall〔wɔl〕*n.* 牆壁

      question〔'kwɛstʃən〕*n.* 問題

      mark〔mɑrk〕*n.* 記號   ***question mark*** 問號

Part B

16. (**C**) What's your special today?

    A. Thank you, but it's nothing.

    B. I'll have that, too.

    C. It's lasagna.   D. It's Tuesday.

    * special (ˈspɛʃəl) *n.* 特餐   have (hæv) *v.* 吃

      lasagna (ləˈzænjə) *n.* 義大利式滷汁麵條（形狀寬而扁，

        上澆肉末、乳酪、蕃茄汁等）

      Tuesday (ˈtjuzde) *n.* 星期二

17. (**A**) Did you remember to bring your ticket?

    A. Here it is.   B. How much is it?

    C. No, I don't know when I bought it.

    D. Yes, I remember him.

    * remember (rɪˈmɛmbɚ) *v.* 記得

      bring (brɪŋ) *v.* 帶來   ***Here it is.*** 在這裡。

18. (**C**) Where can I find an envelope?

    A. It was in the mailbox.

    B. What's the address?

    C. Try the stationery store.

    D. That'll be 85 cents.

    * envelope (ˈɛnvə,lop) *n.* 信封

      mailbox (ˈmel,baks) *n.* 郵筒；信箱

      address (əˈdrɛs, ˈædrɛs) *n.* 地址

      stationery store 文具店   cent (sɛnt) *n.* 分

19. (**B**) Would you like anything to drink with that?

A. Some ketchup, please.

B. No, that's all.

C. I'd like to have it well-done.

D. With cream and sugar.

* ketchup (ˈkɛtʃəp) *n.* 蕃茄醬　　***that's all*** 就這樣
well-done (ˈwɛlˈdʌn) *adj.* 全熟的
cream (krim) *n.* 奶油　　sugar (ˈʃugɚ) *n.* 糖

20. (**D**) Where did you grow up?

A. When I was eighteen.

B. No, my sister is.

C. I'm 180 centimeters.

D. In Taipei.

* ***grow up*** 長大　　centimeter (ˈsɛntə,mitɚ) *n.* 公分
Taipei (ˈtaɪˈpe) *n.* 台北

21. (**D**) Do you know how to start this machine?

A. I started here two months ago.

B. It's a vacuum cleaner.

C. It's Phil's.

D. Turn the key first.

* start (start) *v.* 起動；發動　　machine (məˈʃin) *n.* 機器
vacuum (ˈvækjuəm) *n.* 眞空
cleaner (ˈklinɚ) *n.* 吸塵器
vacuum cleaner 眞空吸塵器　　turn (tɜn) *v.* 轉
key (ki) *n.* 鑰匙　　first (fɜst) *adv.* 首先

22. (**A**) Isn't Rachel a friend of yours?

    A. Yes, she is.

    B. No, she's my friend.

    C. Yes, Mary and Rachel are friends.

    D. Of course you are.

    * Rachel〔'retʃəl〕 *n.* 瑞秋　　*of course* 當然

23. (**C**) What do you plan to do tomorrow?

    A. I'll put it on my calendar.

    B. That sounds good.

    C. I'll probably see a movie.

    D. Yes, I have to do it.

    * plan〔plæn〕 *v.* 計劃　　put〔put〕 *v.* 寫上
      calendar〔'kæləndɚ〕 *n.* 日曆
      sound〔saund〕 *v.* 聽起來
      probably〔'prɑbəblɪ〕 *adv.* 可能

24. (**C**) When did you graduate?

    A. From Taiwan University.

    B. I'm an English major.

    C. Last year.

    D. Yes, I'll go to graduate school.

    * graduate〔'grædʒu,et〕 *v.* 畢業
      Taiwan〔'taɪ'wɑn〕 *n.* 台灣
      university〔,junə'vɝsətɪ〕 *n.* 大學
      major〔'medʒɚ〕 *n.* 主修學生
      graduate school 研究所

25. (**A**) Did you use to play baseball?

    A. Yes, when I was a kid.

    B. Yes, I used it.   C. I put back in the box.

    D. Sure, let's do it.

    * ***used to*** 以前   **play** 〔 ple 〕 *v.* 打 (球)
      baseball 〔'bes,bɔl 〕 *n.* 棒球   **kid** 〔 kɪd 〕 *n.* 小孩
      use 〔 juz 〕 *v.* 使用   ***put back*** 把 (東西) 放回原處
      box 〔 baks 〕 *n.* 盒子   **sure** 〔 ʃur 〕 *adv.* 好；當然

26. (**C**) What was the homework assignment for today?

    A. Yes, I just finished it.

    B. No, it's due tomorrow.

    C. We had to read Chapter Four.

    D. I'm sure she'll assign something.

    * **homework** 〔'hom,wɝk 〕 *n.* 家庭作業
      assignment 〔 ə'saɪnmənt 〕 *n.* 指派；作業
      just 〔 dʒʌst 〕 *adv.* 剛剛   **finish** 〔'fɪnɪʃ 〕 *v.* 完成
      due 〔 du 〕 *adj.* 到期的
      chapter 〔'tʃæptɚ 〕 *n.* (書籍、論文的) 章
      sure 〔 ʃur 〕 *adj.* 確定的   **assign** 〔 ə'saɪn 〕 *v.* 分派；指派

27. (**B**) What were you doing when I called?

    A. Sure, I can do it.   B. Watching television.

    C. I do the housework.

    D. I'll answer it in a minute.

    * **housework** 〔'haus,wɝk 〕 *n.* 家事
      answer 〔'ænsɚ 〕 *v.* 回答   ***in a minute*** 馬上；立刻

28. (**B**) Here's your order.

    A. I'll have the chicken.

    B. Thanks. That was quick.

    C. Yes, you may.

    D. No, I'm the younger one.

    * order ('ɔrdɚ) *n.* 餐點   chicken ('tʃɪkɪn) *n.* 雞肉
      quick (kwɪk) *adj.* 快的
      young (jʌŋ) *adj.* 年輕的

29. (**D**) How much time do you spend playing video games?

    A. Sorry, but I don't have time right now.

    B. It costs NT$30 per hour.

    C. I spend around 300 a week.

    D. About two hours a day.

    * spend (spɛnd) *v.* 花費 (時間、金錢)
      video game 電視玩具   *right now* 現在
      cost (kɔst) *v.* 需要 (…金額)
      per (pɚ) *prep.* 每…   around (ə'raʊnd) *adv.* 大約

30. (**B**) What does Mr. Lee do?

    A. Nice to meet you, too.

    B. He's a salesman.

    C. Fine, thank you.

    D. He does a very good job.

    * *What does sb. do?* 某人是做什麼的？
      salesman ('selzmən) *n.* 售貨員   *do a good job* 做得好

Part C

31. (**B**) M : We definitely need a new sofa. This one really looks old.

W : I think we need all new furniture.

M : Don't get carried away. Let's remember the budget.

Question : What does the man mean?

A. The woman is not capable of carrying the sofa.

B. They have a limited amount of money.

C. Their friend Buddy will give them some furniture.

D. They only need to move the furniture, not replace it.

* definitely (ˈdɛfənɪtlɪ) *adv.* 一定;肯定地
   sofa (ˈsofə) *n.* 沙發　　furniture (ˈfɝnɪtʃɚ) *n.* 傢俱
   get carried away 沖昏頭　　budget (ˈbʌdʒɪt) *n.* 預算
   capable (ˈkepəbl) *adj.* 有能力的　　*be capable of* 能夠
   carry (ˈkærɪ) *v.* 搬運　　limited (ˈlɪmɪtɪd) *adj.* 有限的
   amount (əˈmaunt) *n.* 金額
   move (muv) *v.* 移動　　replace (rɪˈples) *v.* 更換

32. (**D**) W : Did you have any trouble getting to work today?

M : No. Why? Did you?

W : Yes. Highway 5 was backed up for miles!

M : I guess I'm lucky I live in the other direction.

Question : Which of the following statements is true?

A. The man lives further away than the woman.

B. The woman lives five miles from her office.

C. The woman took the highway back to her home.

D. Both the man and the woman drive to work.

* trouble〔'trʌbḷ〕*n.* 困難
  have trouble (*in*) + *V-ing* 很難~　　***get to work*** 去上班
  highway〔'haɪ,we〕*n.* 公路　　***back up*** (交通) 堵塞
  mile〔maɪl〕*n.* 英哩　　guess〔gɛs〕*v.* 猜
  the other 另一個　　direction〔də'rɛkʃən〕*n.* 方向
  following〔'faloɪŋ〕*adj.* 以下的
  statement〔'stetmənt〕*n.* 敘述
  further〔'fɝðə〕*adv.* 更遠；更遠

33. (**A**)　M：How much did your stereo cost you?

W：It was NT$12,000, but I think it's come down a lot since then.

M：When did you buy it?

W：About six months ago.　I should have waited.

Question：What does the woman mean?

A. She would have saved money if she had bought the stereo later.

B. She should have waited for the man to buy the stereo.

C. She spent NT$12,000 too much for the stereo.

D. The man should calm down before he buys a stereo.

* stereo〔'stɛrɪo〕*n.* 音響　　cost〔kɔst〕*v.* 使花費
  come down (價格) 下跌　　since〔sɪns〕*prep.* 自從
  then〔ðɛn〕*n.* 那時　　wait〔wet〕*v.* 等
  save〔sev〕*v.* 省下　　later〔'letə〕*adv.* 後來
  calm down 冷靜

34. (**C**) W: What did the doctor say about your cough?

M: He says it's not a virus or anything like that.

W: So what's causing it?

M: He's not sure, but he wants me to give up smoking.

Question : Why does the doctor want the man to quit
smoking?

A. The woman asked him to.

B. He has a virus.

C. It may be causing his cough.

D. He doesn't allow smoking in the office.

* cough〔kɔf〕*n.* 咳嗽　　virus〔'vaɪrəs〕*n.* 病毒
cause〔kɔz〕*v.* 導致　　***give up*** 放棄
smoke〔smok〕*v.* 吸煙　　quit〔kwɪt〕*v.* 停止；放棄
quit smoking 戒煙 (= *give up smoking*)
ask〔æsk〕*v.* 要求　　allow〔ə'laʊ〕*v.* 允許
office〔'ofɪs〕*n.* 辦公室

35. (**D**) M: Do you have a minute? I'd like to talk to you about
my research project.

W: Sure. Why don't we grab a cup of coffee in the
cafeteria?

M: Sounds good. It'll be my treat.

W: That's not necessary, but thank you.

Question : What does the woman mean?

A. She doesn't like coffee.

B. She does not need to know about the project.

C. The coffee is very good.

D. She does not expect the man to pay for her.

* ***Do you have a minute?*** 你有空嗎？
   research〔'rɪsɝtʃ〕 n. 研究　　project〔'prɑdʒɛkt〕 n. 計畫
   grab〔græb〕 v. 抓住；趕；匆忙地做
   coffee〔'kɔfɪ〕 n. 咖啡
   grab a cup of coffee 匆忙喝杯咖啡
   cafeteria〔ˌkæfə'tɪrɪə〕 n. 自助餐廳
   sound〔saʊnd〕 v. 聽起來　　treat〔trit〕 n. 請客
   necessary〔'nɛsəˌsɛrɪ〕 adj. 必要的
   expect〔ɪk'spɛkt〕 v. 期待　　pay〔pe〕 v. 付錢

36. (**B**)　W：Oh, no! I just broke my mirror!
   M：You know what that means — seven years bad luck.
   W：Oh, don't be silly.
   M：It's not silly. Everybody knows breaking a mirror
       is bad luck.

   Question：Which word best describes the man?

   A. Scary.　　　　　　　　B. Superstitious.
   C. Scarred.　　　　　　　D. Suspicious.

* break〔brek〕 v. 打破　　mirror〔'mɪrɚ〕 n. 鏡子
   bad〔bæd〕 adj. 壞的　　luck〔lʌk〕 n. 運氣
   silly〔'sɪlɪ〕 adj. 愚蠢的
   everybody〔'ɛvrɪˌbɑdɪ〕 pron. 每個人
   word〔wɝd〕 n. 單字　　best〔bɛst〕 adv. 最佳地
   describe〔dɪ'skraɪb〕 v. 描述
   scary〔'skɛrɪ〕 adj. 可怕的；提心吊膽的
   superstitious〔ˌsupɚ'stɪʃəs〕 adj. 迷信的
   scarred〔skɑrd〕 adj. 留下傷痕的
   suspicious〔sə'spɪʃəs〕 adj. 可疑的

37. (**A**) M : Isn't there a bridge over the river?

W : Not for another ten miles. It'll be much faster to take the car ferry.

M : OK, but I warn you that I get seasick easily.

Question : What is true about the man?

A. He does not like boats.

B. He has the flu.

C. He is not in a hurry.

D. The bridge is too far.

* bridge〔brɪdʒ〕n. 橋　　over〔'ovɚ〕prep. 在…上面
　river〔'rɪvɚ〕n. 河　　mile〔maɪl〕n. 英哩
　ferry〔'fɛrɪ〕n. 渡輪
　car ferry 車輛渡輪（運送汽車的渡輪）
　warn〔wɔrn〕v. 警告；提醒
　seasick〔'si,sɪk〕adj. 暈船的　　boat〔bot〕n. 船
　flu〔flu〕n. 流行性感冒（= *influenza*）
　have the flu 患流行性感冒　　*in a hurry* 匆忙地
　far〔far〕adj. 遠的

38. (**B**) W : Do you think it's OK to swim here?

M : I don't see any no swimming signs.

W : I don't see any lifeguards either.

M : Then let's go to the public beach.

Question : Why don't they want to swim there?

A. No one else is swimming there.

B. They think it's not safe enough.

C. It's not allowed.

D. They saw someone guarding the beach.

* ***no swimming*** 禁止游泳　　sign〔saɪn〕*n.* 標誌；告示
   lifeguard〔'laɪf,gɑrd〕*n.* 救生員
   either〔'iðə〕*adv.* 也【用於否定句】
   public〔'pʌblɪk〕*adj.* 公共的　　beach〔bitʃ〕*n.* 海灘
   else〔ɛls〕*adj.* 其它的　　safe〔sef〕*adj.* 安全的
   enough〔ə'nʌf〕*adv.* 足夠地
   allow〔ə'lau〕*v.* 允許　　guard〔gɑrd〕*v.* 看守

39. (C)　M：Brrr. It's chilly today! Do you know the temperature?

W：No, but I guess it's around zero.

M：Maybe we'll get some snow tonight.

W：I doubt it. It's too dry.

Question：What is the most likely weather forecast?

A. Spicy.　　　　　　　　B. Cool and snowy.

C. Freezing temperatures.

D. Hot and dry.

* brrr〔br-rr〕*interj.*【表示冷顫】呵；哦
   chilly〔'tʃɪlɪ〕*adj.* 寒冷的
   temperature〔'tɛmprətʃə〕*n.* 溫度
   guess〔gɛs〕*v.* 猜測　　around〔ə'raund〕*adv.* 大約
   zero〔'zɪro〕*n.* 零；零度　　snow〔sno〕*n.* 雪
   doubt〔daut〕*v.* 懷疑　　dry〔draɪ〕*adj.* 乾燥的
   likely〔'laɪklɪ〕*adj.* 可能的　　weather〔'wɛðə〕*n.* 天氣
   forecast〔'for,kæst〕*n.* 預測；預報
   weather forecast 天氣預報　　spicy〔'spaɪsɪ〕*adj.* 辣的
   cool〔kul〕*adj.* 涼爽的　　snowy〔'snoɪ〕*adj.* 下雪的
   freezing〔'frizɪŋ〕*adj.* 嚴寒的

40. (**C**) W: Can you make out this word?

　　　　　M: No, sorry. Who wrote that anyway?

　　　　　W: I did, but I can't read it, either!

　　　Question : What is the woman's problem?

　　　A. She cannot read.

　　　B. She forgot to write something down.

　　　C. She has bad handwriting.

　　　D. She is nearsighted.

　　　* ***make out*** 認出　　word〔wɜd〕*n.* 字
　　　　anyway〔'ɛnɪ,we〕*adv.* 不管怎樣
　　　　read〔rid〕*v.* 看懂　　forget〔fə'gɛt〕*v.* 忘記
　　　　write down 把…寫下來
　　　　handwriting〔'hænd,raɪtɪŋ〕*n.* 筆跡
　　　　nearsighted〔'nɪr'saɪtɪd〕*adj.* 近視的

41. (**B**) M: Let me help you with those chairs.

　　　　　W: Thanks a lot.

　　　　　M: Where are you taking them?

　　　　　W: The conference room. We have some unexpected
　　　　　　　guests today.

　　　Question : What is going to happen?

　　　A. A dinner party.

　　　B. A meeting.

　　　C. A housewarming party.

　　　D. A furniture sale.

＊ *help sb. with sth.* 幫助某人某事
conference（'kɑnfərəns）*n.* 會議（= *meeting*）
conference room 會議室
unexpected（,ʌnɪk'spɛktɪd）*adj.* 出乎意料的
guest（gɛst）*n.* 客人　　happen（'hæpən）*v.* 發生
dinner party 晚宴　　meeting（'mitɪŋ）*n.* 會議
housewarming（'haʊs,wɔrmɪŋ）*n.* 遷入新居的慶宴
furniture（'fɜnɪtʃə）*n.* 家具　　sale（sel）*n.* 出售；拍賣

42.（ **B** ）W: Did you finish writing all your Christmas cards?

M: Yes, but I'm just sending e-cards this year.

W: I guess you save a lot of money on postage.

M: Sure, but more importantly I know that they'll all
　　 get there on time.

Question : Why did the man send e-cards?

A. Postage is too expensive.

B. They will arrive before Christmas.

C. It was faster to write them.

D. He has more time this Christmas.

＊ finish（'fɪnɪʃ）*v.* 完成
Christmas（'krɪsməs）*n.* 聖誕節　　card（kɑrd）*n.* 卡片
Christmas card 耶誕卡　　just（dʒʌst）*adv.* 只
send（sɛnd）*v.* 寄　　*e-card* 電子卡片
save（sev）*v.* 節省　　postage（'postɪdʒ）*n.* 郵資
importantly（ɪm'pɔrtntlɪ）*adv.* 重要地
more importantly 更重要的是　　*on time* 準時
expensive（ɪk'spɛnsɪv）*adj.* 昂貴的
arrive（ə'raɪv）*v.* 到達

43. (**D**)　M : Let's go to a movie tomorrow.

　　　W : Good idea.　Where should I meet you?

　　　M : How about the coffee shop across the street from the theater?

　　　W : All right.　I'll get tickets for the 3:00 show, and I'll see you there about a quarter of.

　　Question : What time will they meet?

　　A.　At the coffee shop.

　　B.　At three o'clock.

　　C.　Tomorrow morning.

　　D.　2:45 p.m.

　* *go to a movie* 去看電影
　　 idea〔aɪ'diə〕*n.* 主意；想法
　　 meet〔mit〕*v.* 和～見面
　　 How about~? ～如何？　　*coffee shop* 咖啡店
　　 across〔ə'krɔs〕*prep.* 在…的那一邊
　　 street〔strit〕*n.* 街　　theater〔'θiətə〕*n.* 戲院
　　 All right. 好的。　　get〔gɛt〕*v.* 買
　　 show〔ʃo〕*n.* 電影　　quarter〔'kwɔrtə〕*n.* 十五分鐘
　　 a quarter of 十五分鐘前
　　 p.m.〔'pi'ɛm〕*adv.* 下午（= *pm* = *P.M.* = *PM*）

44. (**C**)　W : Wait!　You can't make a left turn here!

　　　M : Why not?

　　　W : The sign says "no left during school hours".

　　　M : But today is a holiday.

Question : Can the man make a turn?

A. Yes, because he is turning left.

B. No, because he will get a ticket.

C. Yes, because children are not in school.

D. No, because it is 6 p.m.

* left〔lɛft〕adj. 左邊的　　*make a turn* 轉彎
  Why not? 爲什麼不？　　say〔se〕v. 說；寫著
  school hours 上學時間
  holiday〔'hɑlə,de〕n. 假日
  turn left 左轉　　ticket〔'tɪkɪt〕n. 罰單

45.(**D**) M: Why are you felling that tree?

W: We're afraid it might hit the house if there's
another big typhoon.

M: That's a shame. It's such a lovely, big tree.

W: Yes, but safety first.

Question : What is happening to the tree?

A. It is dangerous.　　　B. It is falling down.

C. It is being moved.　　D. It is being cut down.

* fell〔fɛl〕v. 砍倒（樹）　　afraid〔ə'fred〕adj. 擔心的
  hit〔hɪt〕v. 擊中；打中　　typhoon〔taɪ'fun〕n. 颱風
  shame〔ʃem〕n. 可惜的事
  lovely〔'lʌvlɪ〕adj. 可愛地；美麗地
  safety〔'seftɪ〕n. 安全　　*safety first* 安全第一
  dangerous〔'dendʒərəs〕adj. 危險的　　*fall down* 倒下
  move〔muv〕v. 移動　　*cut down* 砍伐

English Listening Comprehension Test
Test Book No. 4

This listening comprehension test will test your ability to understand spoken English. In this test, each conversation, statement and question will be spoken JUST ONE TIME. They will not be written out for you. There are three parts to this test. Special instructions will be given to you at the beginning of each part.

Part A

In Part A, you will see several pictures in your test book. For each picture, you will be asked 1 to 3 questions. For each question, you will hear four possible answers. Choose the best answer according to what you see in the picture.

Example:

You will see:

You will hear: What is this?
 A. This is a table.
 B. This is a chair.
 C. This is a watch.
 D. This is a doll.

The best answer to the question "What is this?" is B: "This is a chair." Therefore, you should choose answer B.

A. **Questions 1-3**

B. **Questions 4-5**

C. <u>Questions 6-8</u>

D. <u>Questions 9-11</u>

E. Questions 12-14

F. Question 15

Part B

In Part B, you will hear 15 questions. After you hear a question, read the four possible answers in your test book and decide which one is the best answer to the question you have heard.

Example:

You will hear: What does your father do?

You will read: A. He's 50 years old.

B. He's a teacher.

C. He's hungry.

D. He's in Los Angeles.

The best answer to the question "What does your father do?" is B: "He's a teacher." Therefore, you should choose answer B.

16. A. Wednesday.

B. Yes, it's overcast.

C. Sunny and cool.

D. Yes, it's the fourth.

17. A. I hear her, too.

B. Yes, I've met Susan.

C. She called me yesterday.

D. No, I was on time.

18. A. Thirty-five dollars.
    B. They'll be adults at eighteen.
    C. We have twenty left.
    D. They're for row 28.

19. A. I'll have some, too.
    B. With ice?
    C. Aisle two.
    D. It's $2.89.

20. A. It's English.
    B. Eight a.m.
    C. On Monday morning.
    D. It's an hour and a half.

21. A. I'll graduate next year.
    B. Let's go to a KTV.
    C. In about five years.
    D. A nurse.

22. A. It's a steak.
    B. I'm sorry, ma'am.
    C. It's only $5.99.
    D. Don't mention it.

23. A. It goes to Kaohsiung.
    B. They often have concerts there.
    C. It's in the refrigerator.
    D. On the second floor.

24. A. It's a Rolex.
    B. It's a game show.
    C. It's ten o'clock.
    D. I caught a cold.

25. A. No, it takes at least an hour to get there.
    B. There it goes.
    C. We'll make it.
    D. That's too expensive.

26. A. There's a discount between two and five p.m.
   B. No, I'm not afraid.
   C. Sorry, I have a meeting.
   D. The room is free now.

27. A. Yes, it's just right.
   B. Oh, there's plenty for me.
   C. No, I think I need a bigger spoon.
   D. Yes, I can carry it.

28. A. OK. I'll call around six.
   B. Here you are.
   C. I'm not sure when I'll get them.
   D. Drop by any time.

29. A. About ten kilos.
   B. The line is two blocks long.
   C. It will be ten minutes before we can seat you.
   D. The river is over a thousand kilometers long.

30. A. I live near the train station.
   B. The red house on the corner.
   C. The tall man is our waiter.
   D. The woman by the door.

Part C

In Part C, you will hear 15 conversations between a man and a woman. After each conversation, you will hear a question about the conversation. After you hear the question, read the four possible answers in your test book and choose the best answer to the question you have heard.

Example:

You will hear: (Man)   How do you go to school every day?

(Woman)   Usually by bus. Sometimes by taxi.

Question: How does the woman go to school?

You will read: A. She always goes to school on foot.
B. She usually rides a bike.
C. She takes either a bus or a taxi.
D. She usually goes to school by bus, never by taxi.

The best answer to the question "How does the woman go to school?" is C: "She takes either a bus or a taxi." Therefore, you should choose answer C.

31. A. The boy is not tall.
    B. The boy is not the man's son.
    C. The boy is over 12.
    D. The child is not a boy.

32. A. Put on a jacket.
    B. Swallow medicine.
    C. Be careless.
    D. Find something.

33. A. A ballpark.
    B. An amusement park.
    C. A video game parlor.
    D. A racetrack.

34. A. A pizza parlor.
    B. A sushi bar.
    C. A cafeteria.
    D. A vegetarian restaurant.

35. A. Discuss ice cream.
    B. They are zookeepers.
    C. Make ice cream.
    D. They are vendors.

36. A. She bought some cupcakes.
    B. She sent flowers to Wendy.
    C. She had a bouquet delivered.
    D. She gave the man a special gift.

37. A. Yes, you should take a half-week tour.
    B. No, don't start the tour on Saturday.
    C. Yes, Tuesday and Wednesday are the best days.
    D. No, Monday is not the best day.

38. A. Return in three weeks.
    B. Take the fourth book home.
    C. Read the books in the library.
    D. Do her research.

39. A. News programs.
    B. Reality shows.
    C. Variety shows.
    D. Fictional shows.

40. A. Go bird watching.
    B. Exercise in the early
       morning.
    C. Listen to music.
    D. Sing songs.

41. A. Seven.
    B. No more than one
       month.
    C. As many as he needs
       as long as he is really
       sick.
    D. Five.

42. A. Yesterday.
    B. Around lunchtime.
    C. At 2:00.
    D. In the late afternoon.

43. A. A marine park.
    B. Whale watching.
    C. Fishing.
    D. A restaurant.

44. A. Deliver Gloria's
       message.
    B. Remind the woman to
       call Gloria.
    C. Leave a message.
    D. Place a call to Gloria.

45. A. She has to wait a long
       time, so she may as
       well fill out the form.
    B. She may well fill out
       the form if she has the
       time.
    C. She does not have
       enough time to fill out
       the form.
    D. She cannot fill out the
       form in time.

Listening Test 4 詳解

Part A

For questions number 1 to 3, please look at picture A.

1. (**C**) What is the date?

A. Fish.   B. A bear.

C. October 23rd.   D. On a rock.

* date〔det〕n. 日期　　fish〔fɪʃ〕n. pl. 魚

bear〔bɛr〕n. 熊　　October〔ɑk'tobə〕n. 十月

rock〔rɑk〕n. 岩石

2. (**B**) Please look at picture A again. Where are the fish?

A. The bear caught them.

B. In a pile.

C. There are at least ten.

D. They have been eaten.

* catch〔kætʃ〕v. 抓住

pile〔paɪl〕n. 一堆　　*at least* 至少

3. (**A**) Please look at picture A again. What is on the wall?

A. A calendar.   B. It is winter.

C. A cave.   D. In his mouth.

* wall〔wɔl〕n. 牆壁　　calendar〔'kæləndə〕n. 日曆

winter〔'wɪntə〕n. 冬天　　cave〔kev〕n. 洞穴

mouth〔mauθ〕n. 嘴巴

For questions number 4 and 5, please look at picture B.

4. (**C**)　What is the woman's condition?

　　　　A. She is a housewife.　　B. She is tired.

　　　　C. She is pregnant.　　　D. She is sitting.

　　　* condition (kən'dɪʃən) *n.* 情況
　　　　housewife ('haʊs,waɪf) *n.* 家庭主婦
　　　　tired (taɪrd) *adj.* 疲倦的
　　　　pregnant ('prɛgnənt) *adj.* 懷孕的

5. (**A**)　Please look at picture B again.　What is the man trying
　　　　to do?

　　　　A. Cheer her up.　　　　B. Take her temperature.

　　　　C. Clean the sofa.　　　D. Stop crying.

　　　* try (traɪ) *v.* 嘗試；努力　　　cheer (tʃɪr) *v.* 振作；鼓勵
　　　　cheer sb. up 使人振作
　　　　temperature ('tɛmprətʃɚ) *n.* 溫度
　　　　take one's temperature 量某人的體溫
　　　　clean (klin) *v.* 打掃；清潔　　sofa ('sofə) *n.* 沙發
　　　　stop (stɑp) *v.* 停止　　cry (kraɪ) *v.* 哭泣

For questions number 6 to 8, please look at picture C.

6. (**C**)　What is the woman holding?

　　　　A. Cooking.　　　　　B. A beverage.

　　　　C. A jar.　　　　　　D. Angry.

　　　* hold (hold) *v.* 握住；拿著　　cook (kʊk) *v.* 煮
　　　　beverage ('bɛvərɪdʒ) *n.* 飲料　　jar (dʒɑr) *n.* 廣口瓶
　　　　angry ('æŋgrɪ) *adj.* 生氣的

7. (**A**) Please look at picture C again. How does she feel?

　　 A. Disappointed.　　　 B. It is heavy.

　　 C. Thrilled.　　　　　 D. She is sweating.

　　 * feel〔fil〕v. 覺得

　　 disappointed〔,dɪsə'pɔɪntɪd〕adj. 失望的

　　 heavy〔'hɛvɪ〕adj. 重的（↔ light）

　　 thrilled〔θrɪld〕adj. 非常興奮的；極爲激動的

　　 sweat〔swɛt〕v. 流汗

8. (**D**) Please look at picture C again. What did the man do?

　　 A. He is talking.

　　 B. He is her boyfriend.

　　 C. He is a businessman.

　　 D. He gave her a gift.

　　 * talk〔tɔk〕v. 說話

　　 boyfriend〔'bɔɪ,frɛnd〕n. 男朋友

　　 businessman〔'bɪznɪs,mæn〕n. 商人

　　 gift〔gɪft〕n. 禮物

For questions number 9 to 11, please look at picture D.

9. (**D**) What are the children doing?

　　 A. At school.　　　　 B. In a restaurant.

　　 C. Opening presents.　 D. Eating lunch.

　　 * restaurant〔'rɛstərənt〕n. 餐廳

　　 present〔'prɛznt〕n. 禮物

10. (**A**) Please look at picture D again. What does the girl have?

    A. Chicken.   B. A cake.

    C. McDonald's.   D. A party.

    * chicken〔'tʃɪkən〕n. 雞肉
     cake〔kek〕n. 蛋糕
     McDonald's〔mək'dɑnl̩dz〕n. 麥當勞
     party〔'pɑrtɪ〕n. 宴會

11. (**D**) Please look at picture D again. What is in the girl's hand?

    A. She is waving.   B. A present.

    C. A lunchbox.   D. Chopsticks.

    * wave〔wev〕v. 揮手
     lunchbox〔'lʌntʃ,bɑks〕n. 便當
     chopsticks〔'tʃɑp,stɪks〕n. pl. 筷子

For questions number 12 to 14, please look at picture E.

12. (**C**) What are the man and woman doing?

    A. Shopping.

    B. He is a seller.

    C. Bargaining.

    D. In a market.

    * shop〔ʃɑp〕v. 購物   seller〔'sɛlɚ〕n. 出售者
     bargain〔'bɑrgɪn〕v. 討價還價
     market〔'mɑrkɪt〕n. 市場

13. (**C**) Please look at picture E again. Who is in the
background?

    A. A table.   B. Some vegetables.

    C. Her daughter.   D. The vendor.

    * background (ˈbækˌgraʊnd) *n.* 背景；遠景
      vegetable (ˈvɛdʒtəbḷ) *n.* 蔬菜
      daughter (ˈdɔtɚ) *n.* 女兒
      vendor (ˈvɛndɚ) *n.* 小販

14. (**C**) Please look at picture E again. How much does the
man want?

    A. 50 vegetables.   B. 10 carrots.

    C. 50 dollars.   D. More customers.

    * carrot (ˈkærət) *n.* 胡蘿蔔
      dollar (ˈdɑlɚ) *n.* 元
      customer (ˈkʌstəmɚ) *n.* 顧客

For question number 15, please look at picture F.

15. (**B**) How does the girl feel?

    A. Friendly.   B. Nervous.

    C. Shy.   D. Excited.

    * friendly (ˈfrɛndlɪ) *adj.* 友善的
      nervous (ˈnɜvəs) *adj.* 緊張的
      shy (ʃaɪ) *adj.* 害羞的
      excited (ɪkˈsaɪtɪd) *adj.* 興奮的

Part B

16. (**C**) What's the weather forecast for tomorrow?

    A. Wednesday.   B. Yes, it's overcast.

    C. Sunny and cool.   D. Yes, it's the fourth.

   * weather〔ˈwɛðɚ〕 *n.* 天氣   forecast〔ˈforˌkæst〕 *n.* 預報
    Wednesday〔ˈwɛnzde〕 *n.* 星期三
    overcast〔ˈovɚˌkæst〕 *adj.*（天空）多雲的；陰暗的
    sunny〔ˈsʌnɪ〕 *adj.* 陽光充足的
    cool〔kul〕 *adj.* 涼爽的   fourth〔forθ〕 *n.* 第四

17. (**C**) I haven't heard from Susan lately. How about you?

    A. I hear her, too.   B. Yes, I've met Susan.

    C. She called me yesterday.

    D. No, I was on time.

   * ***hear from*** 得到～的消息   lately〔ˈletlɪ〕 *adv.* 最近
    How about you? 那你呢？   hear〔hɪr〕 *v.* 聽到
    meet〔mit〕 *v.* 和…見面   call〔kɔl〕 *v.* 打電話給
    on time 準時

18. (**A**) How much would two adult tickets be?

    A. Thirty-five dollars.

    B. They'll be adults at eighteen.

    C. We have twenty left.

    D. They're for row 28.

   * adult〔əˈdʌlt〕 *adj.* 成人的   ticket〔ˈtɪkɪt〕 *n.* 入場券；票
    adult ticket 全票；成人票   left〔lɛft〕 *adj.* 剩下的
    row〔ro〕 *n.* 排

19. (**C**) Where can I find the tomato sauce?
    A. I'll have some, too.   B. With ice?
    C. Aisle two.   D. It's $2.89.

  * tomato〔tə'meto〕*n.* 蕃茄
    sauce〔sɔs〕*n.* 醬   have〔hæv〕*v.* 吃
    ice〔aɪs〕*n.* 冰   aisle〔aɪl〕*n.* 通道

20. (**B**) What time is your first class?
    A. It's English.   B. Eight a.m.
    C. On Monday morning.   D. It's an hour and a half.

  * class〔klæs〕*n.* 課
    a.m.〔'e'ɛm〕*adv.* 上午 (= am = A.M. = AM)
    Monday〔'mʌnde〕*n.* 星期一
    an hour and a half 一個半小時

21. (**D**) What would you like to be in the future?
    A. I'll graduate next year.   B. Let's go to a KTV.
    C. In about five years.   D. A nurse.

  * future〔'fjutʃɚ〕*n.* 未來   ***in the future*** 將來
    graduate〔'grædʒu‚et〕*v.* 畢業
    nurse〔nɝs〕*n.* 護士

22. (**B**) Excuse me, but I didn't order this.
    A. It's a steak.   B. I'm sorry, ma'am.
    C. It's only $5.99.   D. Don't mention it.

  * order〔'ɔrdɚ〕*v.* 點 (菜)   steak〔stek〕*n.* 牛排
    ma'am〔mæm〕*n.* 小姐；太太
    mention〔'mɛnʃən〕*v.* 提到   ***Don't mention it.*** 不客氣。

23. (**D**) Where is platform six?

    A. It goes to Kaohsiung.

    B. They often have concerts there.

    C. It's in the refrigerator.

    D. On the second floor.

    * platform (ˈplætˌfɔrm) *n.* 月台　　***Kaohsiung*** 高雄
      often (ˈɔfən) *adv.* 常常　　have (hæv) *v.* 舉辦
      concert (ˈkɑnsɝt) *n.* 音樂會
      refrigerator (rɪˈfrɪdʒəˌretɚ) *n.* 冰箱 (= *fridge*)
      floor (flor) *n.* 樓層

24. (**B**) What are you watching?

    A. It's a Rolex.　　　　B. It's a game show.

    C. It's ten o'clock.　　　D. I caught a cold.

    * Rolex (ˈrolɛks) *n.* 勞力士【手錶品牌】
      game show （電視的）遊戲節目　　***catch a cold*** 感冒

25. (**C**) The train leaves in five minutes!

    A. No, it takes at least an hour to get there.

    B. There it goes.

    C. We'll make it.

    D. That's too expensive.

    * train (tren) *n.* 火車　　leave (liv) *v.* 離開；出發
      minute (ˈmɪnɪt) *n.* 分　　take (tek) *v.* 花費（時間）
      at least 至少　　get (gɛt) *v.* 到達
      There it goes. 它走了。　　***make it*** 趕上
      expensive (ɪkˈspɛnsɪv) *adj.* 昂貴的

26. (**C**) Are you free this afternoon?

    A. There's a discount between two and five p.m.

    B. No, I'm not afraid.   C. Sorry, I have a meeting.

    D. The room is free now.

    * free〔fri〕*adj.*（人）有空的；（場所）空著的
       discount〔'dɪskaʊnt〕*n.* 折扣；減價
       between〔bə'twin〕*prep.* 在…之間
       p.m.〔'pi'ɛm〕*adv.* 下午（= *pm* = *P.M.* = *PM*）
       afraid〔ə'fred〕*adj.* 害怕的   meeting〔'mitɪŋ〕*n.* 會議

27. (**A**) Is your soup hot enough?

    A. Yes, it's just right.

    B. Oh, there's plenty for me.

    C. No, I think I need a bigger spoon.

    D. Yes, I can carry it.

    * soup〔sup〕*n.* 湯   enough〔ə'nʌf〕*adv.* 足夠地
       just right 剛好的   plenty〔'plɛntɪ〕*n.* 很多
       need〔nid〕*v.* 需要   spoon〔spun〕*n.* 湯匙
       carry〔'kærɪ〕*v.* 搬運

28. (**A**) Give me a ring when you get there.

    A. OK. I'll call around six.

    B. Here you are.

    C. I'm not sure when I'll get them.

    D. Drop by any time.

    * ring〔rɪŋ〕*n.* 鈴聲   *give sb. a ring* 打電話給某人
       around〔ə'raʊnd〕*adv.* 大約
       Here you are. 你要的東西在這裡；拿去吧。
       drop by 順道拜訪   *any time* 任何時候

29. (**C**) Do you know how long the wait is?

    A. About ten kilos.

    B. The line is two blocks long.

    C. It will be ten minutes before we can seat you.

    D. The river is over a thousand kilometers long.

    * ***how long*** 多久   wait〔wet〕*n.* 等待；等待的時間
      kilo〔ˈkɪlo〕*n.* 公里；公斤   line〔laɪn〕*n.* 行列
      block〔blɑk〕*n.* 街區   minute〔ˈmɪnɪt〕*n.* 分鐘
      seat〔sit〕*v.* 使～就座   river〔ˈrɪvɚ〕*n.* 河
      over〔ˈovɚ〕*prep.* 超過
      kilometer〔ˈkɪləˌmitɚ〕*n.* 公里

30. (**D**) Which one is your neighbor?

    A. I live near the train station.

    B. The red house on the corner.

    C. The tall man is our waiter.

    D. The woman by the door.

    * neighbor〔ˈnebɚ〕*n.* 鄰居
      near〔nɪr〕*prep.* 在…的附近
      train station 火車站   corner〔ˈkɔrnɚ〕*n.* 轉角
      waiter〔ˈwetɚ〕*n.* 服務生   by〔baɪ〕*prep.* 在…旁邊

Part C

31. (**C**) M: Two adults and two children for the 6:00 show, please.

    W: Uh, is your boy under 12?

    M: Yes, he is. He's tall for his age.

Question : What does the ticket seller think?

A. The boy is not tall.

B. The boy is not the man's son.

C. The boy is over 12.

D. The child is not a boy.

* adult〔 ə'dʌlt 〕*n.* 成人　　show〔 ʃo 〕*n.* 表演；演出
under〔'ʌndə 〕*prep.* (年齡) 低於；未滿
age〔 edʒ 〕*n.* 年紀　　seller〔'sɛlə 〕*n.* 出售者
ticket seller 售票員　　think〔 θɪŋk 〕*v.* 想；認爲
son〔 sʌn 〕*n.* 兒子　　over〔'ovə 〕*prep.* 超過
child〔 tʃaɪld 〕*n.* 小孩

32. (**B**) W: How's your cold today?

M: Better, thanks. I took something for it.

W: Good. But you should still be careful.

M: Don't worry, I will.

Question : What did the man do?

A. Put on a jacket.　　B. Swallow medicine.

C. Be careless.　　D. Find something.

* cold〔 kold 〕*n.* 感冒
better〔'bɛtə 〕*adj.* (病情、身體的感覺) 較好的
take〔 tek 〕*v.* 服用 (藥)　　still〔 stɪl 〕*adv.* 仍然
careful〔'kɛrfəl 〕*adj.* 小心的　　worry〔'wɜɪ 〕*v.* 擔心
put on 穿上　　jacket〔'dʒækɪt 〕*n.* 夾克
swallow〔'swɑlo 〕*v.* 吞下
medicine〔'mɛdəsn̩ 〕*n.* 藥
careless〔'kɛrlɪs 〕*adj.* 粗心的

33. (**A**)　M : It looks like it could rain. Do you offer rain checks
　　　　　　if that happens?

　　　　W : We do if the game is stopped by the seventh inning.

　　　　M : OK. Four bleacher seats, please.

　　　　Question : Where does this conversation take place?

　　　　A. A ballpark.　　　　　　B. An amusement park.
　　　　C. A video game parlor.　　D. A racetrack.

　　* ***look like*** 看起來像　　　rain〔ren〕v. 下雨
　　　offer〔'ɔfɚ〕v. 提供　　***rain check*** 因雨延期入場憑證
　　　happen〔'hæpən〕v. 發生　　game〔gem〕n. 比賽
　　　stop〔stɑp〕v. 中斷；停止　　by〔baɪ〕prep. 在…之前
　　　inning〔'ɪnɪŋ〕n.（棒球）局
　　　bleacher〔'blitʃɚ〕n. 外野席　　seat〔sit〕n. 座位
　　　conversation〔,kɑnvɚ'seʃən〕n. 對話
　　　take place 發生　　ballpark〔'bɔl,park〕n. 球場
　　　amusement〔ə'mjuzmənt〕n. 消遣；娛樂
　　　amusement park 遊樂園　　***video game*** 電動玩具
　　　parlor〔'parlɚ〕n. 店
　　　racetrack〔'res,træk〕n. 賽車場；賽馬場

34. (**A**)　W : What can I get you?

　　　　M : We'll have a medium seafood. How many pieces
　　　　　　is that?

　　　　W : Eight slices, sir. It's usually enough for two people.

　　　　M : Fine. And is the salad bar included?

　　　　W : Yes. Just help yourselves.

Question : What kind of restaurant is this?

A. A pizza parlor.

B. A sushi bar.

C. A cafeteria.

D. A vegetarian restaurant.

* get〔gɛt〕v. 取來；拿
medium〔'midɪəm〕adj. 中等的
seafood〔'si,fud〕n. 海鮮　　piece〔pis〕n. 片
slice〔slaɪs〕n. 片　　usually〔'juʒʊəlɪ〕adv. 通常
salad〔'sæləd〕n. 沙拉　　*salad bar* 沙拉吧
include〔ɪn'klud〕v. 包含
help oneself 自行取用　　kind〔kaɪnd〕n. 種類
restaurant〔'rɛstərənt〕n. 餐廳
pizza〔'pitsə〕n. 披薩　　*pizza parlor* 披薩店
sushi〔'susɪ〕n. 壽司　　*sushi bar* 壽司吧
cafeteria〔,kæfə'tɪrɪə〕n. 自助餐廳
vegetarian〔,vɛdʒə'tɛrɪən〕adj. 素食的

35. (**D**) M : How much ice cream did you order?

W : Ten liters each of vanilla and chocolate.

M : That may not be enough. Tomorrow is a holiday,
　　so it's sure to be a busy day at the zoo.

W : Then I'll order another five liters of each plus
　　some strawberry.

Question : What do the speakers do?

A. Discuss ice cream.

B. They are zookeepers.

C. Make ice cream.

D. They are vendors.

* ice cream (ˈaɪsˈkrim) n. 冰淇淋
order (ˈɔrdɚ) v. 訂購　　liter (ˈlitɚ) n. 公升
vanilla (vəˈnɪlə) n. 香草
chocolate (ˈtʃɔklɪt) n. 巧克力
holiday (ˈhɑləˌde) n. 假日
busy (ˈbɪzɪ) adj. 忙碌的　　zoo (zu) n. 動物園
another (əˈnʌðɚ) adj. 另一個；又一的
each (itʃ) adv. 每個　　plus (plʌs) prep. 加上
strawberry (ˈstrɔˌbɛrɪ) n. 草莓
speaker (ˈspikɚ) n. 說話者
discuss (dɪˈskʌs) v. 討論
zookeeper (ˈzuˌkipɚ) n. 動物園管理員
vendor (ˈvɛndɚ) n. 小販

36. (**C**)　W: Hello. I'd like to order some flowers.

　　　　M: Would you like our Monday morning special? It's
　　　　　　a small bouquet of buttercups for $12.95.

　　　　W: That sounds fine. Please send it to 123 Second
　　　　　　Avenue, apartment 2B.

　　　　M: Your name?

　　　　W: Wendy Holmes.

　　　　Question : What did the woman do?

A. She bought some cupcakes.

B. She sent flowers to Wendy.

C. She had a bouquet delivered.

D. She gave the man a special gift.

* **would like** 想要　　order (ˈɔrdɚ) v. 訂購
  special (ˈspɛʃəl) n. 特價品
  bouquet (buˈke) n. 花束
  buttercup (ˈbʌtɚˌkʌp) n. 毛茛
  sound (saʊnd) v. 聽起來　　send (sɛnd) v. 寄；送
  avenue (ˈævəˌnju) n. 大街；大道
  apartment (əˈpɑrtmənt) n. 公寓
  cupcake (ˈkʌpˌkek) n. 杯形蛋糕
  deliver (dɪˈlɪvɚ) v. 遞送　　gift (gɪft) n. 禮物

37. (**C**)　M: Hi. We're interested in your seven-day European tour. Could you explain why there are different prices?

W: The price depends on your day of departure. We can get a better deal with the airlines if we avoid flying on a weekend.

M: I see. So it would be best to book a trip that starts mid-week?

Question : What will the woman's answer most likely be?

A. Yes, you should take a half-week tour.

B. No, don't start the tour on Saturday.

C. Yes, Tuesday and Wednesday are the best days.

D. No, Monday is not the best day.

* ***be interested in*** 對…有興趣

  European〔ˌjurəˈpiən〕 *adj.* 歐洲的

  tour〔tur〕 *n.* 旅行

  explain〔ɪkˈsplen〕 *v.* 說明；解釋

  different〔ˈdɪfərənt〕 *adj.* 不同的

  price〔praɪs〕 *n.* 價格　　***depend on*** 視…而定

  departure〔dɪˈpartʃɚ〕 *n.* 出發　　deal〔dil〕 *n.* 交易

  airlines〔ˈɛrˌlaɪnz〕 *n. pl.* 航空公司

  avoid〔əˈvɔɪd〕 *v.* 避開　　fly〔flaɪ〕 *v.* 飛行

  weekend〔ˈwikˌɛnd〕 *n.* 週末　　***I see.*** 我了解了。

  book〔buk〕 *v.* 預訂　　trip〔trɪp〕 *n.* 旅程

  start〔start〕 *v.* 起程；出發

  mid〔mɪd〕 *adj.* …中間的　　answer〔ˈænsɚ〕 *n.* 回答

  likely〔ˈlaɪklɪ〕 *adj.* 可能的　　***half-week*** 半週的

38. (**B**) W: I'd like to check out these books.

    M: I'm sorry, but this one may be read in the library only.

    W: No problem. I'll just take these three then. When are they due?

    M: In three weeks.

    Question: What can't the woman do?

A. Return in three weeks.

B. Take the fourth book home.

C. Read the books in the library.

D. Do her research.

* **check out** 辦理借（書）手續

library（'laɪˌbrɛrɪ）n. 圖書館　　only（'onlɪ）adv. 僅；只

then（ðɛn）adv. 那麼　　due（du）adj. 到期的

return（rɪ'tɜn）v. 歸還　　research（'risɜtʃ）n. 研究

39.（ **B** ）M：What kind of TV programs do you like to watch?

W：I like all kinds of reality shows — you know,

　　Survivor, *The Bachelor*, and so on.

M：Don't you think they're kind of fake?

W：Maybe, but they're still fun to watch.

Question：What does the woman like to watch?

A. News programs.　　　B. Reality shows.

C. Variety shows.　　　　D. Fictional shows.

* kind（kaɪnd）n. 種類　　program（'progræm）n. 節目

reality（rɪ'ælətɪ）n. 真實　　**reality show** 實境節目

survivor（sə'vaɪvə）n. 生還者

bachelor（'bætʃələ）n. 單身漢　　**and so on** 等等

kind of 有點　　fake（fek）adj. 假的

maybe（'mebi）adv. 可能　　fun（fʌn）adj. 有趣的

news（njuz）n. 新聞

variety（və'raɪətɪ）adj. 綜藝節目的

variety show 綜藝節目　　fictional（'fɪkʃənl）adj. 虛構的

40. (**A**) W: What are you listening to?

M: The birdsong. The early morning is the best time.

W: So that's why you always go out so early.

M: Yes. I've spotted a wide variety of species so far.

Question : What does the man like to do?

A. Go bird watching.

B. Exercise in the early morning.

C. Listen to music.

D. Sing songs.

* ***listen to*** 聽   birdsong〔'bɝd͵sɔŋ〕*n.* 鳥鳴
always〔'ɔlwez〕*adv.* 總是   ***go out*** 出去
spot〔spɑt〕*v.* 認出;發現
wide〔waɪd〕*adj.* 廣的;廣泛的
variety〔və'raɪətɪ〕*n.* 各式各樣
a wide variety of 很多各式各樣的
species〔'spiʃɪz〕*n.* 物種;種類
so far 到目前為止   ***bird watching*** 賞鳥
exercise〔'ɛksə͵saɪz〕*v.* 運動
music〔'mjuzɪk〕*n.* 音樂
sing〔sɪŋ〕*v.* 唱(歌)   song〔sɔŋ〕*n.* 歌曲

41. (**D**) M: How many sick days does your company allow
you to take?

W: Five, officially, but they'll allow more if you
don't abuse the privilege.

M : What if you have to miss a lot of work — let's say, a month?

W : They don't have to cover more than a week, but it really depends on your situation.

Question : How many days can an employee take sick leave and still be sure of getting paid?

A. Seven.

B. No more than one month.

C. As many as he needs as long as he is really sick.

D. Five.

* *sick day* 病假　　company (ˈkʌmpənɪ) *n.* 公司

　allow (əˈlaʊ) *v.* 准許

　take (tek) *v.* 享有；得到（休息、休假）

　officially (əˈfɪʃəlɪ) *adv.* 正式地

　abuse (əˈbjuz) *v.* 濫用

　privilege (ˈprɪvlɪdʒ) *n.* 特權

　What if~? 如果～該怎麼辦？

　miss (mɪs) *v.* 錯過；遺漏　　*a lot of* 很多

　let's say 例如　　month (mʌnθ) *n.* 月

　cover (ˈkʌvɚ) *v.* 支付【在此指「支付薪水」】

　really (ˈrɪəlɪ) *adv.* 真正地

　situation (ˌsɪtʃʊˈeʃən) *n.* 情況

　employee (ˌɛmplɔɪˈi) *n.* 員工

　take sick leave 請病假　　*be sure of* 確定

　get paid 有薪資　　*no more than* 不超過

　as many as 和～一樣多　　*as long as* 只要

42. (**B**) W: Did you know that tomorrow's meeting has been moved up?

M: No. When's it going to happen?

W: This afternoon. Two o'clock.

M: What? That gives me only a couple of hours to prepare!

Question: When did this conversation take place?

A. Yesterday.

B. Around lunchtime.

C. At 2:00.

D. In the late afternoon.

* meeting〔'mitɪŋ〕n. 會議　*move up* 提前
  happen〔'hæpən〕v. 發生；舉行
  a couple of 幾個　prepare〔prɪ'pɛr〕v. 準備；預備
  conversation〔,kɑnvɚ'seʃən〕n. 對話
  take place 發生
  lunchtime〔'lʌntʃ,taɪm〕n. 午餐時間
  late〔let〕adj. 稍晚的

43. (**B**) M: Did you see many whales during your tour?

W: Oh, yes. Lots of them. At least a dozen.

M: Wow. I guess you were lucky.

W: Maybe, but our guide said this is the best time of year to go.

Question: Where did the woman go?

A. A marine park.   B. Whale watching.

C. Fishing.   D. A restaurant.

* whale (hwel) n. 鯨魚   during ('durıŋ) prep. 在…的期間

tour (tur) n. 旅行   *lots of* 很多   *at least* 至少

dozen ('dʌzn̩) n. 一打;十二個

wow (wau) interj. 哇;啊   guess (gɛs) v. 猜

lucky ('lʌkı) adj. 運氣好的   guide (gaɪd) n. 導遊

the best time of year to~ 一年中做~最好的時機

marine (mə'rin) adj. 海洋的   *marine park* 海洋公園

whale watching 賞鯨   fishing ('fıʃıŋ) n. 釣魚

restaurant ('rɛstərənt) n. 餐廳

44. (**D**) W: Gloria called you again.

M: What did she want?

W: She didn't say, but she wants you to call her back
right away. It sounded urgent.

M: Well, then. I guess we'd better do it.

Question : What will the man most likely do?

A. Deliver Gloria's message.

B. Remind the woman to call Gloria.

C. Leave a message.

D. Place a call to Gloria.

* again (ə'gɛn) adv. 再;又   *call sb. back* 回電話給某人

right away 馬上;立刻   sound (saund) v. 聽起來

urgent ('ɝdʒənt) adj. 緊急的   *had better V.* 最好~

deliver (dı'lıvɚ) v. 遞送   message ('mɛsıdʒ) n. 訊息

remind (rı'maınd) v. 提醒   *leave a message* 留言

place a call to~ 打電話給~

45. (**A**) M : Please fill out this form while you wait for the doctor. He'll be with you in about half an hour.

W : But I'm not a new patient. Don't you have all this information already?

M : Yes, but we have new requirements from the insurance company, so I need some additional information.

W : All right. It's not like I don't have the time.

Question : What does the woman mean?

A. She has to wait a long time, so she may as well fill out the form.

B. She may well fill out the form if she has the time.

C. She does not have enough time to fill out the form.

D. She cannot fill out the form in time.

* ***fill out*** 填寫　　form〔fɔrm〕*n.* 表格
while〔hwaɪl〕*conj.* 當…的時候　　***wait for*** 等待
patient〔'peʃənt〕*n.* 病人
information〔͵ɪnfɚ'meʃən〕*n.* 資料
already〔ɔl'rɛdɪ〕*adv.* 已經
requirements〔rɪ'kwaɪrmənts〕*n. pl.* 要求；必備條件
insurance〔ɪn'ʃurəns〕*n.* 保險
company〔'kʌmpənɪ〕*n.* 公司
additional〔ə'dɪʃənl̩〕*adj.* 額外的　　***All right***. 好吧。
like〔laɪk〕*prep.* 像　　mean〔min〕*v.* 意思是
may as well 不妨　　***may well*** 大可以；很有理由
in time 及時

English Listening Comprehension Test
Test Book No. 5

This listening comprehension test will test your ability to understand spoken English. In this test, each conversation, statement and question will be spoken JUST ONE TIME. They will not be written out for you. There are three parts to this test. Special instructions will be given to you at the beginning of each part.

Part A

In Part A, you will see several pictures in your test book. For each picture, you will be asked 1 to 3 questions. For each question, you will hear four possible answers. Choose the best answer according to what you see in the picture.

Example:

<u>You will see</u>:

<u>You will hear</u>:   What is this?
   A. This is a table.
   B. This is a chair.
   C. This is a watch.
   D. This is a doll.

The best answer to the question "What is this?" is B: "This is a chair." Therefore, you should choose answer B.

A. <u>Questions 1-3</u>

B. <u>Questions 4-6</u>

C. <u>Questions 7-8</u>

D. <u>Questions 9-10</u>

E. Questions 11-13

F. Questions 14-15

Part B

In Part B, you will hear 15 questions. After you hear a question, read the four possible answers in your test book and decide which one is the best answer to the question you have heard.

Example:

You will hear: What does your father do?

You will read: A. He's 50 years old.
B. He's a teacher.
C. He's hungry.
D. He's in Los Angeles.

The best answer to the question "What does your father do?" is B: "He's a teacher." Therefore, you should choose answer B.

16. A. Medium or
well-done?
B. Right away.
C. I'm your waiter.
D. Here's your check.

17. A. There is one-hour parking
across the street.
B. Yes, but you have to put
some money in the meter.
C. Sure. But only on a leash.
D. I don't know who they
belong to.

18. A. That'll be $12.95.
    B. Can I see the dessert menu?
    C. No, I didn't care for it.
    D. I care a lot about the environment.

19. A. It's a Japanese language tape.
    B. Sorry. I wasn't paying attention.
    C. I studied classical music.
    D. I'm trying to read that sign across the street.

20. A. No, that'll be all.
    B. I'm going to the library.
    C. Here you are.
    D. We'll have it here.

21. A. The Harry Potter books are my favorite.
    B. We have to write a two-page essay.
    C. Twenty — that's most of chapter one.
    D. I read a book every month.

22. A. I was offered a job yesterday.
    B. I'm looking for Baker Street.
    C. No luck so far.
    D. I'm going there now.

23. A. For a business conference.
    B. Last July.
    C. About a week.
    D. It's my favorite city.

24. A. No, I never learned how.
    B. Only when there is a lifeguard on duty.
    C. It costs NT$100.
    D. It's 5:00.

25. A. Every half hour.
    B. It's only 50 kilometers from here.
    C. It's arriving now.
    D. About two hours.

26. A. Life is a dream.
    B. Not on your life!
    C. You can say that again.
    D. You are too polite.

27. A. No, I was born on the fifteenth.
    B. Yes, I'll be twenty-three.
    C. Yes, but not clearly.
    D. No, I'll definitely be there.

28. A. Yes, I must to.
    B. No, I needn't.
    C. Yes, I have.
    D. No, I should to.

29. A. Just a little black pepper, please.
    B. I like the news on channel 12.
    C. I love the summer.
    D. Yes, I have a great reason.

30. A. No, thanks. I'm full.
    B. Yes, I ever did.
    C. No, I'm afraid of heights.
    D. Yes, I've tried yoga.

Part C

In Part C, you will hear 15 conversations between a man and a woman. After each conversation, you will hear a question about the conversation. After you hear the question, read the four possible answers in your test book and choose the best answer to the question you have heard.

Example:

<u>You will hear</u>: (Man)　　How do you go to school every day?

　　　　　　　 (Woman)　Usually by bus. Sometimes by taxi.

　　　　　　　 Question:　How does the woman go to school?

<u>You will read</u>:　A. She always goes to school on foot.

　　　　　　　 B. She usually rides a bike.

　　　　　　　 C. She takes either a bus or a taxi.

　　　　　　　 D. She usually goes to school by bus, never by taxi.

The best answer to the question "How does the woman go to school?" is C: "She takes either a bus or a taxi." Therefore, you should choose answer C.

31. A. Around $125 per night.
    B. At least $95.
    C. $245.
    D. $95 a night or $150 a week.

32. A. A barbecue.
    B. A ride to the store.
    C. A fire extinguisher.
    D. Some matches.

33. A. On a train.
    B. On an airplane.
    C. In an office.
    D. In a library.

34. A. Earlier today.
    B. Before he goes home.
    C. At 3:00.
    D. On Friday.

35. A. He will eat whatever is left of his owners' dinner.
    B. His owners will cook a special meal for him.
    C. He will go out for dinner.
    D. He will get only a little food.

36. A. A second orange soda.
    B. As much orange soda as she likes.
    C. A receipt for her meal.
    D. A coupon for a free drink.

37. A. He will take a taxi.
    B. He will drive as fast as possible.
    C. That depends on his driver.
    D. He will take the highway.

38. A. The elevator is always very crowded.
    B. The elevator is hard to use.
    C. Most people use the moving stairways.
    D. The woman doesn't know how to use a stairway.

39. A. Get a discount.
    B. Get on the plane.
    C. Buy a train ticket.
    D. Wait for the next departure.

40. A. She is the man's adopted sister.
    B. She is the man's sister-in-law.
    C. She is not a member of the man's family.
    D. She is a friend of the man's sisters.

41. A. She buys a newspaper.
    B. She reads fashion magazines.
    C. She has no time for the news.
    D. She reads it once a week.

42. A. He worked in the library.
    B. He played many sports, but not well.
    C. He read a lot.
    D. He was not very popular.

43. A. Just before 5:00.
    B. At home.
    C. In the evening.
    D. In an office.

44. A. He is trying to lose weight.
    B. He has a toothache.
    C. The desserts are not good.
    D. He is not fond of sweets.

45. A. The man should do further research.
    B. The man should talk to a company representative.
    C. The man should invest in the field.
    D. The man should invest only at the high end.

Listening Test 5 詳解

Part A

For questions number 1 to 3, please look at picture A.

1. (**A**) What does the man do?
   A. He sells fish.
   B. He looks like a fish.
   C. He has large ears.
   D. He is a cook.

   * sell〔sɛl〕*v.* 賣　　fish〔fɪʃ〕*n. pl.* 魚
   look like 看起來像　　large〔lɑrdʒ〕*adj.* 大的
   ear〔ɪr〕*n.* 耳朵　　cook〔kʊk〕*n.* 廚師

2. (**C**) Please look at picture A again. What is the woman doing?
   A. She is whistling.
   B. She is whispering.
   C. She is telling the boy to be quiet.
   D. She is telling the boy he cannot have a fish.

   * whistle〔'hwɪsl̩〕*v.* 吹口哨
   whisper〔'hwɪspɚ〕*v.* 低聲地說
   tell〔tɛl〕*v.* 告訴
   quiet〔'kwaɪət〕*adj.* 安靜的　　have〔hæv〕*v.* 擁有

3. (**B**) Please look at picture A again. What is the boy carrying?

    A. He cares about fish.

    B. A pet fish.

    C. A lunchbox.

    D. To his mother.

    * carry〔'kærɪ〕v. 提；拿　　***care about*** 擔心

      pet〔pɛt〕adj. 作寵物的

      lunchbox〔'lʌntʃ,bɑks〕n. 便當

For questions number 4 to 6, please look at picture B.

4. (**C**) What day is it?

    A. Valentine's Day.

    B. Halloween.

    C. The girl's birthday.

    D. Their first date.

    * valentine〔'væləntaɪn〕n. 情人節禮物

      Valentine's Day 情人節

      Halloween〔,hælo'in〕n. 萬聖節前夕（即十月三十一日晚上）

      birthday〔'bɝθ,de〕n. 生日　　date〔det〕n. 約會

5. (**A**) Please look at picture B again. What does the boy have?

    A. A gift.　　　　　　　　B. A flower.

    C. A birthday.　　　　　　D. A bird.

    * gift〔gɪft〕n. 禮物

6. (**C**) Please look at picture B again. How does she feel?

    A. Embarrassed.

    B. Nervous.

    C. Furious.

    D. Hot.

    * feel (fil) v. 覺得

      embarrassed (ɪm'bærəst) adj. 尷尬的

      nervous ('nɜvəs) adj. 緊張的

      furious ('fjʊrɪəs) adj. 狂怒的   hot (hɑt) adj. 熱的

For questions number 7 and 8, please look at picture C.

7. (**C**) Whose dish is it?

    A. A mouse.

    B. Food.

    C. The cat's.

    D. On the floor.

    * dish (dɪʃ) n. 菜餚;食物   mouse (maʊs) n. 老鼠

      floor (flor) n. 地板

8. (**A**) Please look at picture C again. What is the girl doing?

    A. Watching.

    B. Cooking.

    C. On the floor.

    D. She is happy.

    * watch (wɑtʃ) v. 注視   cook (kʊk) v. 煮

For questions number 9 and 10, please look at picture D.

9. (**B**) When does this happen?

    A. In the bedroom.

    B. At Christmas.

    C. The boy has been good.

    D. It's his birthday.

    * happen〔'hæpən〕v. 發生　bedroom〔'bɛd,rum〕n. 臥房
    Christmas〔'krɪsməs〕n. 聖誕節　good〔gud〕adj. 乖的

10. (**D**) Please look at picture D again. What is the boy

       dreaming about?

    A. Santa Claus.

    B. In bed.

    C. He is sleeping.

    D. Presents.

    * *dream about* 夢到　*Santa Claus* 耶誕老人
    bed〔bɛd〕n. 床　sleep〔slip〕v. 睡覺
    present〔'prɛzn̩t〕n. 禮物

For questions number 11 to 13, please look at picture E.

11. (**C**) How many boxes are on the floor?

    A. It's a big box.

    B. One.

    C. Five.

    D. They are empty.

    * box〔baks〕n. 盒子；箱子　empty〔'ɛmptɪ〕adj. 空的

12. (**C**) Please look at picture E again. What was in the box?

    A. Nothing.   B. A bow.

    C. A candy.   D. Hearts.

    * bow〔bo〕*n.* 蝴蝶結   candy〔'kændɪ〕*n.* 糖果

     heart〔hɑrt〕*n.* 心臟；心形物

13. (**D**) Please look at picture E again. What did the girl get?

    A. Sad.   B. A Valentine.

    C. Embarrassed.   D. A gift.

    * sad〔sæd〕*adj.* 悲傷的

For questions number 14 and 15, please look at picture F.

14. (**B**) What are the boys doing?

    A. They are racing.   B. Riding motorbikes.

    C. They are cool.   D. Giving a ride.

    * race〔res〕*v.* 賽跑   ride〔raɪd〕*v.* 騎

     motorbike〔'motɚ͵baɪk〕*n.* 摩托車

     cool〔kul〕*adj.* 很酷的   ***give a ride*** 載人

15. (**B**) Please look at picture F again. What is the middle boy wearing?

    A. A helmet.   B. Sunglasses.

    C. A bike.   D. A thumb.

    * middle〔'mɪdl̩〕*adj.* 中間的   wear〔wɛr〕*v.* 穿；戴

     helmet〔'hɛlmɪt〕*n.* 頭盔；安全帽

     sunglasses〔'sʌn͵glæsɪz〕*n. pl.* 太陽眼鏡

     bike〔baɪk〕*n.* 腳踏車   thumb〔θʌm〕*n.* 大姆指

Part B

16. (**B**) Could we have some more water, please?

    A. Medium or well-done?

    B. Right away.

    C. I'm your waiter.

    D. Here's your check.

    * medium ('midɪəm) adj. (牛排)五分熟的
      well-done ('wɛl'dʌn) adj. 全熟的
      Right away. 馬上來。   waiter ('wetɚ) n. 服務生
      check (tʃɛk) n. 帳單

17. (**C**) Are dogs allowed in the park?

    A. There is one-hour parking across the street.

    B. Yes, but you have to put some money in the meter.

    C. Sure. But only on a leash.

    D. I don't know who they belong to.

    * allow (ə'lau) v. 允許…進入
      park (park) n. 公園   v. 停車
      parking ('parkɪŋ) n. 停車位
      one-hour parking 可停車一小時的停車場
      across (ə'krɔs) prep. 在…的那一邊；在…的對面
      street (strit) n. 街道   ***put…in*** 將…投入
      meter ('mitɚ) n. 收費器
      leash (liʃ) n. (拴狗的)鍊子；皮帶
      on a leash 用皮帶拴著的
      belong (bə'lɔŋ) v. 屬於 < *to* >

18. (**B**) Would you care for something else?

    A. That'll be $12.95.

    B. Can I see the dessert menu?

    C. No, I didn't care for it.

    D. I care a lot about the environment.

    * *care for* 想要;喜歡

       else (ɛls) *adj.* 其它的;別的

       That'll be~ 總共~   dessert (dɪ'zɜt) *n.* 甜點

       menu ('mɛnju) *n.* 菜單   *care about* 在意;擔心

       a lot 非常   environment (ɪn'vaɪrənmənt) *n.* 環境

19. (**A**) What are you listening to?

    A. It's a Japanese language tape.

    B. Sorry. I wasn't paying attention.

    C. I studied classical music.

    D. I'm trying to read that sign across the street.

    * listen ('lɪsn̩) *v.* 聽 < *to* >

       Japanese (,dʒæpə'niz) *adj.* 日本的

       language ('læŋgwɪdʒ) *n.* 語言

       tape (tep) *n.* 錄音帶

       attention (ə'tɛnʃən) *n.* 注意(力)

       pay attention 集中注意力

       study ('stʌdɪ) *v.* 學習;研讀

       classical ('klæsɪkl̩) *adj.* 古典的

       music ('mjuzɪk) *n.* 音樂   read (rid) *v.* 查看;判讀

       sign (saɪn) *n.* 告示;標誌

20. (**D**) Is that for here or to go?

    A. No, that'll be all.   B. I'm going to the library.

    C. Here you are.   D. We'll have it here.

    * ***For here or to go?*** 內用或外帶？
    that'll be all 那就是全部   library (ˈlaɪˌbrɛrɪ) *n.* 圖書館
    Here you are. 你要的東西在這裡；拿去吧。
    have (hæv) *v.* 吃

21. (**C**) How many pages have you read?

    A. The Harry Potter books are my favorite.

    B. We have to write a two-page essay.

    C. Twenty — that's most of chapter one.

    D. I read a book every month.

    * page (pedʒ) *n.* 頁   favorite (ˈfevərɪt) *n.* 最喜歡的東西
    essay (ˈɛse) *n.* 論文；文章
    most (most) *pron.* 大部分
    chapter (ˈtʃæptə) *n.* 章   month (mʌnθ) *n.* 月

22. (**C**) How is the apartment search going?

    A. I was offered a job yesterday.

    B. I'm looking for Baker Street.

    C. No luck so far.   D. I'm going there now.

    * ***How's～going?*** ～近況如何？
    apartment (əˈpɑrtmənt) *n.* 公寓
    search (sɜtʃ) *n.* 搜尋；尋找   offer (ˈɔfə) *v.* 提供
    job (dʒɑb) *n.* 工作   ***look for*** 尋找
    luck (lʌk) *n.* 運氣   ***no luck*** 運氣不好
    so far 到目前為止

23. (**B**) When were you in London?

A. For a business conference.

B. Last July.　　　　C. About a week.

D. It's my favorite city.

* London〔'lʌndən〕*n.* 倫敦

conference〔'kɑnfərəns〕*n.* 會議

business conference 商業會議

favorite〔'fevərɪt〕*adj.* 最喜歡的

24. (**B**) Is swimming allowed here?

A. No, I never learned how.

B. Only when there is a lifeguard on duty.

C. It costs NT$100.　　D. It's 5:00.

* swim〔swɪm〕*v.* 游泳　　allow〔ə'lɑʊ〕*adv.* 允許

never〔'nɛvɚ〕*adv.* 絕不；從未

lifeguard〔'laɪf,gɑrd〕*n.* 救生員

on duty 執勤中　　cost〔kɔst〕*v.* 需要（…金額）

25. (**D**) How long does it take for the train to get to Taipei?

A. Every half hour.

B. It's only 50 kilometers from here.

C. It's arriving now.

D. About two hours.

* **_How long does it take~?_** ～要花多少時間？

get to 到達　　Taipei〔'taɪ'pe〕*n.* 台北

every half hour 每隔半小時

kilometer〔'kɪlə,mitɚ〕*n.* 公里　　arrive〔ə'raɪv〕*v.* 抵達

26. (**B**) Were you ever tempted to jaywalk here?

    A. Life is a dream.

    B. Not on your life!

    C. You can say that again.

    D. You are too polite.

    * ever (ˈɛvə) *adv.* 曾經

      tempt (tɛmpt) *v.* 誘惑　　***be tempted to*** 想要

      jaywalk (ˈdʒe‚wɔk) *v.* 擅自穿越馬路

      dream (drim) *n.* 夢

      Not on your life! 不可能！休想！

      You can say that again. 你說的沒錯。

      polite (pəˈlaɪt) *adj.* 有禮貌的；客氣的

27. (**C**) Can you remember your fifth birthday?

    A. No, I was born on the fifteenth.

    B. Yes, I'll be twenty-three.

    C. Yes, but not clearly.

    D. No, I'll definitely be there.

    * remember (rɪˈmɛmbə) *v.* 記得；想起

      fifth (fɪfθ) *adj.* 第五的　　***be born*** 出生

      the fifteenth 十五日

      clearly (ˈklɪrlɪ) *adv.* 清楚地

      definitely (ˈdɛfənɪtlɪ) *adv.* 絕對；一定

28. (**B**) Do you have to work on the holiday?

    A. Yes, I must to.

    B. No, I needn't.

    C. Yes, I have.

    D. No, I should to.

    * holiday〔'hɑlə,de〕 *n.* 節日;假日

29. (**C**) What's your favorite season?

    A. Just a little black pepper, please.

    B. I like the news on channel 12.

    C. I love the summer.

    D. Yes, I have a great reason.

    * season〔'sizn〕*n.* 季節   pepper〔'pɛpɚ〕*n.* 胡椒（粉）
    black pepper 黑胡椒（粉）   news〔njuz〕*n.* 新聞
    channel〔'tʃænl〕*n.* 頻道   great〔gret〕*adj.* 極好的
    reason〔'rizn〕*n.* 理由

30. (**C**) Would you ever try something like bungee jumping?

    A. No, thanks. I'm full.

    B. Yes, I ever did.

    C. No, I'm afraid of heights.

    D. Yes, I've tried yoga.

    * try〔traɪ〕*v.* 嘗試
    bungee jumping〔'bʌndʒi'dʒʌmpɪŋ〕*n.* 高空彈跳
    full〔fʊl〕*adj.* 吃飽的   ***be afraid of*** 害怕
    heights〔haɪts〕*n. pl.* 高處   yoga〔'jogə〕*n.* 瑜伽

Part C

31. (**B**) M: Do you have any vacancies?

W: Yes, we have one double room available, and one suite.

M: And how much is it?

W: The double is $95 a night and the suite is $150.

Question : How much money must the man spend?

A. Around $125 per night.

B. At least $95.

C. $245.

D. $95 a night or $150 a week.

* vacancy〔'vekənsɪ〕*n.* 空房間

double room 雙人房

available〔ə'veləbḷ〕*adj.* 可獲得的

suite〔swit〕*n.* 套房

spend〔spɛnd〕*v.* 花費（錢）

around〔ə'raʊnd〕*adv.* 大約

per〔pɚ〕*prep.* 每⋯　　**at least** 至少

32. (**D**) W: Did anyone bring matches to light the grill?

M: I think Lee brought some.

W: I hope so. Otherwise, we won't be able to cook our dinner.

M: Oh, someone could always run to the store.

Question : What do they need?

A. A barbecue.

B. A ride to the store.

C. A fire extinguisher.

D. Some matches.

* bring〔brɪŋ〕v. 帶來　　match〔mætʃ〕n. 火柴

light〔laɪt〕v. 點燃　　grill〔grɪl〕n. 烤肉架

I hope so. 希望如此。

otherwise〔ˈʌðəˌwaɪz〕adv. 要不然；否則

be able to V. 能夠～

always〔ˈɔlwez〕adv. 總是

run〔rʌn〕v. 跑　　store〔stor〕n. 商店

barbecue〔ˈbɑrbɪˌkju〕n. 烤肉（= Bar-B-Q）

ride〔raɪd〕n. 搭乘

extinguisher〔ɪkˈstɪŋgwɪʃə〕n. 滅火器

fire extinguisher 滅火器

33. (**D**) M : Is that your phone ringing?

W : No. Mine is right here. Besides, it's turned off.

M : I wish someone would answer it. It's driving me crazy.

W : You're not supposed to use cell phones here anyway. People are trying to study.

Question : Where might this conversation take place?

A. On a train.　　　　B. On an airplane.
C. In an office.　　　　D. In a library.

* phone〔fon〕*n.* 電話（= *telephone*）
ring〔rɪŋ〕*v.*（電話）鈴響　　***right here*** 在這裡
besides〔bɪ'saɪdz〕*adv.* 此外　　***turn off*** 關掉
wish〔wɪʃ〕*v.* 希望　　answer〔'ænsɚ〕*v.* 接（電話）
crazy〔'krezɪ〕*adj.* 瘋狂的　　***drive sb. crazy*** 使人抓狂
be supposed to V. 應該~　　***cell phone*** 手機
anyway〔'ɛnɪ,we〕*adv.* 不管怎樣　　***try to V.*** 想要~
study〔'stʌdɪ〕*v.* 讀書
conversation〔,kɑnvɚ'seʃən〕*n.* 對話　　***take place*** 發生
train〔tren〕*n.* 火車　　airplane〔'ɛr,plen〕*n.* 飛機
office〔'ɔfɪs〕*n.* 辦公室　　library〔'laɪ,brɛrɪ〕*n.* 圖書館

34. (**B**) W: When do you think you'll be finished with that report?
M: I'll have it done today for sure.
W: That's great. Could I have it by three?
M: Let's say the end of the day.

Question: When will the man give the report to the
woman?

A. Earlier today.　　　　B. Before he goes home.
C. At 3:00.　　　　D. On Friday.

* finish〔'fɪnɪʃ〕*v.* 完成　　report〔rɪ'port〕*n.* 報告
done〔dʌn〕*adj.* 完成的　　***for sure*** 一定
great〔gret〕*adj.* 很棒的　　by〔baɪ〕*prep.* 在…之前
let's say 例如；就這麼說吧　　end〔ɛnd〕*n.* 結束
the end of the day（工作等）完成之時
Earlier today. 今天較早的時候。

35. (**A**)　M : Did you remember to buy some more dog food?

　　　　　W : No, I forgot.

　　　　　M : So what are we going to feed Spot?

　　　　　W : Let's just give him table scraps tonight.

　　　Question : What will Spot eat?

　　　A.　He will eat whatever is left of his owners' dinner.

　　　B.　His owners will cook a special meal for him.

　　　C.　He will go out for dinner.

　　　D.　He will get only a little food.

　　　* remember〔rɪ'mɛmbɚ〕v. 記得
　　　　some more 多一點的　　***dog food*** 狗食
　　　　forget〔fɚ'gɛt〕v. 忘記　　feed〔fid〕v. 餵
　　　　scraps〔skræps〕n. pl. 剩餘的食物
　　　　table scraps 剩菜
　　　　whatever〔hwɑt'ɛvɚ〕pron. 任何東西
　　　　left〔lɛft〕adj. 剩下的　　owner〔'onɚ〕n. 主人；擁有者
　　　　special〔'spɛʃəl〕adj. 特別的　　meal〔mil〕n. 一餐
　　　　go out for dinner 出去吃晚餐　　***a little*** 一點點

36. (**A**)　W : Could I get a refill, please?

　　　　　M : Certainly.　What are you drinking?

　　　　　W : Orange soda.　How much is that?

　　　　　M : You get one free refill.

　　　Question : What will the woman get?

A.　A second orange soda.

B.　As much orange soda as she likes.

C.　A receipt for her meal.

D.　A coupon for a free drink.

＊ refill〔'ri,fɪl〕n. 續杯　　certainly〔'sɝtn̩lɪ〕adv. 當然

soda〔'sodə〕n. 汽水　　*orange soda* 橘子汽水

free〔fri〕adj. 免費的　　*a second* 另一個

as much…as 與…一樣多　　receipt〔rɪ'sit〕n. 收據

coupon〔'kupɑn〕n. 折價券

37.（ **D** ）　M：How long will it take to get into the city?

W：That depends on your route.　The highway is faster,
but you'll have to pay some tolls.

M：Oh, that doesn't matter.

Question：How will the man go to the city?

A.　He will take a taxi.

B.　He will drive as fast as possible.

C.　That depends on his driver.

D.　He will take the highway.

＊ *depend on* 視…而定　　route〔rut〕n. 路線

highway〔'haɪ,we〕n. 公路

fast〔fæst〕adj. 快的　　pay〔pe〕v. 支付

toll〔tol〕n. 通行費　　matter〔'mætɚ〕v. 關係重要

as…as possible 儘可能…　　driver〔'draɪvɚ〕n. 司機

take〔tek〕v. 選擇；利用

38. (**C**) W: Excuse me, but where are the elevators?

M: There's one at the end of this hall.

W: Thanks. I never would have known. Why do they make it so hard to find?

M: Well, most people take the escalators, I guess.

Question : What is true?

A. The elevator is always very crowded.

B. The elevator is hard to use.

C. Most people use the moving stairways.

D. The woman doesn't know how to use a stairway.

* elevator (ˈɛləˌvetɚ) n. 電梯；升降梯

end (ɛnd) n. 盡頭；末端   hall (hɔl) n. 走廊

I never would have known. 要不然我永遠都不會知道。

(= *I would not have known where the elevator is if you hadn't told me.*)

hard (hɑrd) adj. 困難的   take (tek) v. 搭乘

escalator (ˈɛskəˌletɚ) n. 手扶梯   guess (gɛs) v. 猜

crowded (ˈkraʊdɪd) adj. 擁擠的

moving (ˈmuvɪŋ) adj. 會移動的

stairway (ˈstɛrˌwe) n. 樓梯   ***moving stairway*** 手扶梯

39. (**C**) M: Are there any seats left on the 5:30 to Boston?

W: Sorry, there aren't. But you can always stand.

M: Is the price the same?

W: Yes, there's just one ticket price.

M: All right, then.

Question : What will the man do?

A. Get a discount.　　B. Get on the plane.

C. Buy a train ticket.

D. Wait for the next departure.

* seat〔sit〕*n.* 座位　　left〔lɛft〕*adj.* 剩下的

Boston〔'bɔstn̩〕*n.* 波士頓

always〔'ɔlwez〕*adv.* 總是；一直　　stand〔stænd〕*v.* 站著

price〔praɪs〕*n.* 價格　　*the same* 相同的

just〔dʒʌst〕*adv.* 只；僅　　discount〔'dɪskaʊnt〕*n.* 折扣

get on 搭上（交通工具）　　plane〔plen〕*n.* 飛機

wait for 等待　　next〔nɛkst〕*adj.* 下一個的

departure〔dɪ'pɑrtʃɚ〕*n.* 啓程；出發

40.（**B**）W: You have four sisters, don't you?

M: No, only three.　Patty is my brother Tom's wife.

W: Really?　She looks a lot like your sisters!

M: That's 'cause they all have blond hair.

Question : Who is Patty?

A. She is the man's adopted sister.

B. She is the man's sister-in-law.

C. She is not a member of the man's family.

D. She is a friend of the man's sisters.

* wife〔waɪf〕*n.* 老婆　　*a lot* 非常（= *much*）

like〔laɪk〕*prep.* 像

'cause〔kɔz〕*conj.* 因爲（= *because*）

blond〔blɑnd〕*adj.*（頭髮）金色的

adopted〔ə'dɑptɪd〕*adj.* 被領養的

sister-in-law 嫂嫂；弟媳；妯娌

member〔'mɛmbɚ〕*n.* 成員

41. (**A**) M : Do you subscribe to any magazines?

W : Yes, I get a couple of fashion magazines.

M : No news magazines like *Time* or *Newsweek*?

W : No, I'd rather read about that kind of thing in the newspaper.

Question : How does the woman get the news?

A. She buys a newspaper.

B. She reads fashion magazines.

C. She has no time for the news.

D. She reads it once a week.

* subscribe 〔 səb'skraɪb 〕 *v.* 訂閱 < *to* >

magazine 〔 ˌmæɡə'zin 〕 *n.* 雜誌

a couple of 幾個；兩個

fashion 〔 'fæʃən 〕 *n.* 流行；時尚

news 〔 njuz 〕 *n.* 新聞　　*Time* 時代雜誌

Newsweek 美國新聞週刊

would rather 寧願；寧可　　kind 〔 kaɪnd 〕 *n.* 種類

newspaper 〔 'njuz,pepɚ 〕 *n.* 報紙

once 〔 wʌns 〕 *adv.* 一次

42. (**C**) W : What kind of sports did you play in high school?

M : Not many. I was kind of bookish.

W : No sports at all?

M : A little ping-pong, but no football, baseball or anything like that.

Question : What did the man do in high school?

A. He worked in the library.

B. He played many sports, but not well.

C. He read a lot.

D. He was not very popular.

* sport〔sport〕*n.* 運動

play〔ple〕*v.* 打（球）；參加

high school 高中　　***kind of*** 有點

bookish〔'bʊkɪʃ〕*adj.* 喜歡讀書的；書呆子氣的

at all 全然（不…）；一點也（不…）

a little 一點　　ping-pong〔'pɪŋ͵pɑŋ〕*n.* 乒乓球；桌球

football〔'fʊt͵bɔl〕*n.* 橄欖球

baseball〔'bes͵bɔl〕*n.* 棒球

well〔wɛl〕*adv.* 好地　　***a lot*** 很多

popular〔'pɑpjələ〕*adj.* 受歡迎的

43. (**D**) M : Is that clock right?

W : I believe so. Why?

M : I just can't believe it's that late. It's almost time to go home.

W : Yeah. I may try to leave now and beat the evening rush.

Question : Where does this conversation take place?

A. Just before 5:00.　　B. At home.

C. In the evening.　　D. In an office.

* clock〔klɑk〕*n.* 時鐘　　right〔raɪt〕*adj.* 正確的

　believe〔bə'liv〕*v.* 相信　　so〔so〕*adv.* 如此

　late〔let〕*adj.* 晚的　　almost〔'ɔl,most〕*adv.* 幾乎

　It's time to~　　~的時候到了

　yeah〔jæ〕*adv.* 是的（*= yes*）

　beat〔bit〕*v.* 比…搶先　　rush〔rʌʃ〕*n.* 交通尖峰時間

44. (**D**) W：What would you like for dessert? We have apple
　　　　　　pie, cheesecake, and chocolate cake.

　　　　M：Nothing for me, thanks.

　　　　W：Are you sure? They're all very good.

　　　　M：No, thanks. I don't have much of a sweet tooth.

　　　　Question : What does the man mean?

　　　　A. He is trying to lose weight.

　　　　B. He has a toothache.

　　　　C. The desserts are not good.

　　　　D. He is not fond of sweets.

* dessert〔dɪ'zɝt〕*n.* 甜點　　pie〔paɪ〕*n.* 派

　cheesecake〔'tʃiz,kek〕*n.* 起司蛋糕

　chocolate〔'tʃɔklɪt〕*n.* 巧克力

　sweet〔swit〕*adj.* 甜的　　*n.* 甜食

　tooth〔tuθ〕*n.* 牙齒　　*sweet tooth* 嗜吃甜食

　I don't have much of a sweet tooth. 我不是很喜歡吃甜食。

　lose〔luz〕*v.* 減輕（體重）　　weight〔wet〕*n.* 體重

　toothache〔'tuθ,ek〕*n.* 牙痛　　*be fond of* 喜歡

45. (**A**) M: Have you ever heard of this company?

W: Yes. They're a clothing company. They sell to many high-end shops.

M: Do you think it's a good investment?

W: I think you should talk with an expert in the field.

Question : What does the woman suggest?

A. The man should do further research.

B. The man should talk to a company representative.

C. The man should invest in the field.

D. The man should invest only at the high end.

* ***heard of*** 聽說   company (ˈkʌmpənɪ) *n.* 公司

clothing (ˈkloðɪŋ) *n.* 服裝

high-end (ˈhaɪˈɛnd) *adj.* 最高級的；高價位的

  (↔ *low-end* (ˈloˈɛnd) *adj.* 較便宜的)

investment (ɪnˈvɛstmənt) *n.* 投資

expert (ˈɛkspɜt) *n.* 專家   field (fild) *n.* 領域

suggest (səgˈdʒɛst) *v.* 建議

further (ˈfɜðæ) *adj.* 更進一步的

research (riˈsɜtʃ , ˈrisɜtʃ) *v. n.* 研究

representative (ˌrɛprɪˈzɛntətɪv) *n.* 代表

invest (ɪnˈvɛst) *v.* 投資 < *in* >

invest at the high end 投資昂貴的物品

  (= *invest in expensive things*)

English Listening Comprehension Test
Test Book No. 6

This listening comprehension test will test your ability to understand spoken English. In this test, each conversation, statement and question will be spoken JUST ONE TIME. They will not be written out for you. There are three parts to this test. Special instructions will be given to you at the beginning of each part.

Part A

In Part A, you will see several pictures in your test book. For each picture, you will be asked 1 to 3 questions. For each question, you will hear four possible answers. Choose the best answer according to what you see in the picture.

Example:

You will see:

You will hear: What is this?
        A. This is a table.
        B. This is a chair.
        C. This is a watch.
        D. This is a doll.

The best answer to the question "What is this?" is B: "This is a chair." Therefore, you should choose answer B.

A. <u>Questions 1-2</u>

B. <u>Questions 3-5</u>

C. <u>Questions 6-7</u>

D. <u>Questions 8-10</u>

E. <u>Questions 11-12</u>

F. <u>Questions 13-15</u>

Part B

In Part B, you will hear 15 questions. After you hear a question, read the four possible answers in your test book and decide which one is the best answer to the question you have heard.

Example:

<u>You will hear</u>: What does your father do?

<u>You will read</u>: A. He's 50 years old.

B. He's a teacher.

C. He's hungry.

D. He's in Los Angeles.

The best answer to the question "What does your father do?" is B: "He's a teacher." Therefore, you should choose answer B.

16. A. Let me try.

B. At last!

C. Look out!

D. Let's ask.

17. A. It's on sale.

B. I got some shoes.

C. No, it was too expensive.

D. I went this morning.

18. A. It's on the table.
    B. Oh, yes. Here it is.
    C. Go on. Tell me.
    D. When did you do it?

19. A. My friend Sue.
    B. It's mine.
    C. It's on the desk.
    D. I can't find it.

20. A. I have a bad case of
       the flu.
    B. I have to cancel.
    C. It's not serious.
    D. I'll take him to dinner.

21. A. In the Philippines.
    B. The weather was
       terrible!
    C. I took two weeks off.
    D. I'm going to drive.

22. A. No, that's all.
    B. No, just a Coke.
    C. I'll have the number
       two meal.
    D. It's for here.

23. A. I prefer cooler weather.
    B. It's going to be a nice
       day.
    C. I don't know whether
       it's today or tomorrow.
    D. I'd rather go today.

24. A. I like all kinds.
    B. Yes, it's very
       friendly.
    C. It's Mary's dog.
    D. It's a poodle.

25. A. Yes, I would.
    B. It's to go.
    C. With a salad.
    D. Medium-well.

26. A. No, I don't.
    B. No, I'd rather go with you.
    C. I have a headache.
    D. I'm really looking forward to it.

27. A. Pleased to meet you.
    B. Likewise.
    C. How have you been?
    D. Don't mention it.

28. A. We need three of them.
    B. They're NT$50 per kilo.
    C. They're in aisle four.
    D. They weigh 300 grams.

29. A. I have to hand it in by 5:00.
    B. It's a boy.
    C. In November.
    D. Don't worry, I'll take care of him.

30. A. Because I like living there.
    B. No, it's too far.
    C. No, I didn't do it.
    D. Yes, I'll consider it.

Part C

In Part C, you will hear 15 conversations between a man and a woman. After each conversation, you will hear a question about the conversation. After you hear the question, read the four possible answers in your test book and choose the best answer to the question you have heard.

Example:

You will hear: (Man) How do you go to school every day?

(Woman) Usually by bus. Sometimes by taxi.

Question: How does the woman go to school?

You will read: A. She always goes to school on foot.
  B. She usually rides a bike.
  C. She takes either a bus or a taxi.
  D. She usually goes to school by bus, never by taxi.

The best answer to the question "How does the woman go to school?" is C: "She takes either a bus or a taxi." Therefore, you should choose answer C.

31. A. The play wasn't very good.
    B. The theater was too crowded.
    C. The play is worth seeing.
    D. The man was lucky to have a good seat.

32. A. He cut himself.
    B. He played with a sharp knife.
    C. He held a sharp knife near some children.
    D. He put a knife where children could get it.

33. A. An anonymous band.
    B. A popular song.
    C. A new band.
    D. A new play.

34. A. Play games for three hours.
    B. Say that he should study now.
    C. Begin to study now.
    D. Study for a long time.

35. A. It is not noisy.
    B. There is not much to do.
    C. Yes, he likes it very much.
    D. It's the best part of the city.

36. A. Accept the compliment.
    B. Drop the man off at the door.
    C. Pay the valet a compliment.
    D. Let the staff park her car.

37. A. Make the same sweater as the man.
    B. Make everyone knit a sweater.
    C. Give everyone a sweater for Christmas.
    D. Get a job making sweaters.

38. A. The weather is
    unusually warm.
    B. The air conditioner is
    broken.
    C. The repairman sent
    the wrong AC.
    D. The man forgot to
    order an AC.

39. A. She has to meet her
    sister at the resort.
    B. She has presents for
    her sister.
    C. She must carry
    everything herself.
    D. She has gifts for her
    parents and sister.

40. A. In the winter.
    B. To a warm place.
    C. To a ski resort.
    D. Later in the year.

41. A. A traffic ticket.
    B. A jaywalking ticket.
    C. A parking ticket.
    D. A speeding ticket.

42. A. songs.
    B. radios.
    C. volumes.
    D. earphones.

43. A. He placed his
    sunglasses on his face.
    B. He lost two pairs of
    sunglasses.
    C. He broke his sunglasses.
    D. He missed the sunglasses
    twice this week.

44. A. Sit by himself.
    B. Have a party.
    C. Sit by the window.
    D. Smoke in the restaurant.

45. A. Next Monday.
    B. He cannot.
    C. On the weekend.
    D. Every Monday.

Listening Test 6 詳解

Part A

For questions number 1 and 2, please look at picture A.

1. (**D**) What is on the floor?
   A. Yes, they are sitting on it.
   B. They are playing a game.
   C. It is a bedroom.
   D. There are some cards.

   * floor〔flor〕n. 地板　　*play a game* 玩遊戲
     bedroom〔'bɛd,rum〕n. 臥室
     card〔kɑrd〕n. 紙牌

2. (**B**) Please look at picture A again.　What is the girl doing?
   A. She is winning.
   B. She is putting something down.
   C. She is a poor player.
   D. She is on the right.

   * win〔wɪn〕v. 贏;獲勝
     put down 放下
     poor〔pʊr〕adj. 差勁的
     player〔'pleɚ〕n. 玩家
     right〔raɪt〕n. 右邊　　*on the right* 在右邊

For questions number 3 to 5, please look at picture B.

3. (**D**) Why are the rabbits angry?

    A. They are not cats.

    B. They are not hungry.

    C. They are not angry.

    D. They do not like the food.

    * rabbit〔ˈræbɪt〕*n.* 兔子　　angry〔ˈæŋgrɪ〕*adj.* 生氣的

    hungry〔ˈhʌŋgrɪ〕*adj.* 飢餓的

4. (**D**) Please look at picture B again. What is in the bowl?

    A. No, it's a bag.　　　　B. Two rabbits.

    C. A cat.　　　　　　　 D. Cat food.

    * bowl〔bol〕*n.* 碗　　bag〔bæg〕*n.* 袋子

5. (**C**) Please look at picture B again. What is the boy doing?

    A. Shouting at the cats.　　B. Playing.

    C. Raising his arms.　　　　D. Praying.

    * shout〔ʃaut〕*v.* 吼叫　　play〔ple〕*v.* 玩耍

    raise〔rez〕*v.* 舉起　　arm〔ɑrm〕*n.* 手臂

    pray〔pre〕*v.* 祈禱

For questions number 6 and 7, please look at picture C.

6. (**B**) What caught a fish?

    A. They are big fish.　　　B. An octopus.

    C. Three fish.　　　　　　D. It is hungry.

    * catch〔kætʃ〕*v.* 抓住　　octopus〔ˈɑktəpəs〕*n.* 章魚

7. (**C**) Please look at picture C again. How many of the
animal's arms can we see?

    A. Three.   B. Four.

    C. Seven.   D. Eight.

    * animal〔'ænəml̩〕 *n.* 動物

For questions number 8 to 10, please look at picture D.

8. (**B**) Where is the boy standing?

    A. On the wall.

    B. In a puddle.

    C. He is barefoot.

    D. He is screaming.

    * stand〔stænd〕 *v.* 站   wall〔wɔl〕 *n.* 牆壁
      puddle〔'pʌdl̩〕 *n.* 水坑
      barefoot〔'bɛr͵fut〕 *adj.* 赤腳的
      scream〔skrim〕 *v.* 尖叫

9. (**B**) Please look at picture D again. What did the boy do?

    A. He dried his hair.

    B. He shocked himself.

    C. He is surprised.

    D. He mopped the floor.

    * dry〔draɪ〕 *v.* 使變乾   hair〔hɛr〕 *n.* 頭髮
      shock〔ʃak〕 *v.* 使觸電；使震驚
      surprised〔sə'praɪzd〕 *adj.* 驚訝的
      mop〔map〕 *v.* 用拖把拖

10. (**A**) Please look at picture D again. What is in his hand?

        A. An electrical cord.   B. A hairbrush.

        C. Water.   D. An outlet.

      * electrical (ɪˋlɛktrɪkḷ) *adj.* 電的

        cord (kɔrd) *n.* 繩索;電線   ***electrical cord*** 電線

        hairbrush (ˋhɛr͵brʌʃ) *n.* 髮刷;毛刷

        outlet (ˋaʊt͵lɛt) *n.* 插座

For questions number 11 and 12, please look at picture E.

11. (**A**) What is the boy on the left doing?

        A. Diving.   B. Going to the bathroom.

        C. Smiling.   D. Crying.

      * left (lɛft) *n.* 左邊   dive (daɪv) *v.* 潛水

        bathroom (ˋbæθ͵rum) *n.* 浴室;廁所

        smile (smaɪl) *v.* 微笑   cry (kraɪ) *v.* 哭

12. (**C**) Please look at picture E again. Where is the smallest boy?

        A. Under the water.

        B. In a bathing cap.

        C. On the surface.

        D. On a bed.

      * under (ˋʌndɚ) *prep.* 在⋯之下

        bathing (ˋbeðɪŋ) *n.* 沐浴;泡水;游泳

        cap (kæp) *n.* 無邊的帽子   ***bathing cap*** 泳帽

        surface (ˋsɝfɪs) *n.* 表面;水面   bed (bɛd) *n.* 床

For questions number 13 to 15, please look at picture F.

13. (**A**) What is the man around the corner holding?

　　A. A newspaper.　　　　B. The wall.

　　C. Glasses.　　　　　　D. A boy and girl.

　　* corner〔'kɔrnɚ〕*n.* 角落　　***around the corner*** 在轉角
　　　hold〔hold〕*v.* 拿著　　newspaper〔'njuz,pepɚ〕*n.* 報紙
　　　glasses〔'glæsɪz〕*n.* 玻璃杯；眼鏡

14. (**D**) Please look at picture F again. How does the girl wear her hair?

　　A. It is blond.　　　　B. She is embarrassed.

　　C. A dress.　　　　　　D. In a ponytail.

　　* wear〔wɛr〕*v.* 把（頭髮）留成（…狀態）
　　　blond〔blɑnd〕*adj.* 金髮的
　　　embarrassed〔ɪm'bærəst〕*adj.* 尷尬的
　　　dress〔drɛs〕*n.* 洋裝　　ponytail〔'ponɪ,tel〕*n.* 馬尾

15. (**B**) Please look at picture F again. What is the young man doing?

　　A. He is waiting for the man.

　　B. He is bringing the girl.

　　C. He is using sign language.

　　D. He is her father.

　　* young〔jʌŋ〕*adj.* 年輕的　　***wait for*** 等待
　　　bring〔brɪŋ〕*v.* 帶（人）　　use〔juz〕*v.* 使用
　　　sign〔saɪn〕*n.* 手勢；符號
　　　language〔'læŋgwɪdʒ〕*n.* 語言　　***sign language*** 手語

Part B

16. (**B**) Here's the street we're looking for!

    A. Let me try.   B. At last!

    C. Look out!   D. Let's ask.

    * street〔strit〕*n.* 街道   ***look for*** 尋找

    let〔lɛt〕*v.* 讓   try〔traɪ〕*v.* 嘗試

    At last! 終於!   ***Look out!*** 小心!

17. (**B**) What did you buy at the department store?

    A. It's on sale.

    B. I got some shoes.

    C. No, it was too expensive.

    D. I went this morning.

    * ***department store*** 百貨公司   ***on sale*** 特價;拍賣

    get〔gɛt〕*v.* 買   shoe〔ʃu〕*n.* 鞋子

    expensive〔ɪk'spɛnsɪv〕*adj.* 昂貴的

18. (**B**) You'll find the story on page three of the newspaper.

    A. It's on the table.

    B. Oh, yes. Here it is.

    C. Go on. Tell me.

    D. When did you do it?

    * story〔'storɪ〕*n.* 新聞報導;故事

    page〔pedʒ〕*n.* 頁;(報紙的)版面

    newspaper〔'njuz,pepɚ〕*n.* 報紙   ***Here it is.*** 在這裡。

    go on 繼續   tell〔tɛl〕*v.* 告訴

19. (**A**) Who was on the phone?
    A. My friend Sue.   B. It's mine.
    C. It's on the desk.   D. I can't find it.

    * phone (fon) *n.* 電話 (= *telephone*)
      on the phone 電話中;講電話
      Sue (su) *n.* 蘇   desk (dɛsk) *n.* 書桌

20. (**C**) Why don't you make an appointment with Dr. Clark?
    A. I have a bad case of the flu.
    B. I have to cancel.   C. It's not serious.
    D. I'll take him to dinner.

    * appointment (ə'pɔɪntmənt) *n.* (診療等的) 預約
      make an appointment with ~ 與~約定時間
      Dr. ('dɑktɚ) *n.* …醫生 (= *doctor*)
      Clark (klɑrk) *n.* 克拉克   bad (bæd) *adj.* 嚴重的
      case (kes) *n.* (疾病的) 病症;病情
      flu (flu) *n.* 流行性感冒 (= *influenza*)
      cancel ('kænsl̩) *v.* 取消   serious ('sɪrɪəs) *adj.* 嚴重的
      take sb. to dinner 帶某人去吃晚餐

21. (**B**) How was your vacation?
    A. In the Philippines.
    B. The weather was terrible!
    C. I took two weeks off.   D. I'm going to drive.

    * vacation (ve'keʃən) *n.* 假期
      Philippines ('fɪlə,pinz) *n.* 菲律賓
      weather ('wɛðɚ) *n.* 天氣
      terrible ('tɛrəbl̩) *adj.* 極糟糕的   ***take ~ off*** 休假~
      week (wik) *n.* 週   drive (draɪv) *v.* 開車

22. (**A**) Would you like anything to drink with that?

    A. No, that's all.

    B. No, just a Coke.

    C. I'll have the number two meal.

    D. It's for here.

    * ***that's all*** 就這樣；那就是全部
       Coke 〔 kok 〕 *n.* 可口可樂
       number 〔'nʌmbə 〕 *n.* 第 (幾) 號   meal 〔 mil 〕 *n.* 餐

23. (**B**) What's the weather like today?

    A. I prefer cooler weather.

    B. It's going to be a nice day.

    C. I don't know whether it's today or tomorrow.

    D. I'd rather go today.

    * like 〔 laɪk 〕 *prep.* 像
       What's the weather like today? 今天天氣如何？
       prefer 〔 prɪ'fɝ 〕 *v.* 比較喜歡   cool 〔 kul 〕 *adj.* 涼爽的
       nice 〔 naɪs 〕 *adj.* 好的   whether 〔'hwɛðə 〕 *conj.* 是否
       would rather 寧願

24. (**D**) What kind of dog is that?

    A. I like all kinds.

    B. Yes, it's very friendly.

    C. It's Mary's dog.

    D. It's a poodle.

    * kind 〔 kaɪnd 〕 *n.* 種類   friendly 〔'frɛndlɪ 〕 *adj.* 友善的
      poodle 〔'pudl̩ 〕 *n.* 貴賓狗

25. (**D**) How would you like that cooked?

      A. Yes, I would.   B. It's to go.

      C. With a salad.   D. Medium-well.

    * cook〔kʊk〕v. 煮   ***to go*** 外帶
      salad〔'sæləd〕n. 沙拉   ***medium-well*** 七分熟的

26. (**C**) Why don't you want to go with us?

      A. No, I don't.

      B. No, I'd rather go with you.

      C. I have a headache.

      D. I'm really looking forward to it.

    * headache〔'hɛd͵ek〕n. 頭痛
      really〔'riəlɪ〕adv. 真地
      look forward to 期待

27. (**A**) I'd like to introduce my friend Jim.

      A. Pleased to meet you.

      B. Likewise.

      C. How have you been?

      D. Don't mention it.

    * ***would like to V.*** 想要～
      introduce〔͵ɪntrə'djus〕v. 介紹
      pleased〔plizd〕adj. 高興的   meet〔mit〕v. 認識
      likewise〔'laɪk͵waɪz〕adv. 同樣地
      How have you been? 你好嗎？
      Don't mention it. 不客氣。

28. (**B**) How much are the lemons?

    A. We need three of them.

    B. They're NT$50 per kilo.

    C. They're in aisle four.

    D. They weigh 300 grams.

    * lemon〔'lɛmən〕*n.* 檸檬　　need〔nid〕*v.* 需要
      per〔pɚ〕*prep.* 每一　　kilo〔'kɪlo〕*n.* 公斤（= *kilogram*）
      aisle〔aɪl〕*n.* 走道；通道
      weigh〔we〕*v.* 重…　　gram〔græm〕*n.* 公克

29. (**C**) When is the baby due?

    A. I have to hand it in by 5:00.

    B. It's a boy.

    C. In November.

    D. Don't worry. I'll take care of him.

    * baby〔'bebɪ〕*n.* 嬰兒　　due〔du〕*adj.* 到期的；預期的
      hand in 繳交　　by〔baɪ〕*prep.* 在…之前
      November〔no'vɛmbɚ〕*n.* 十一月　　***take care of*** 照顧

30. (**B**) Have you ever considered moving to the suburbs?

    A. Because I like living there.

    B. No, it's too far.

    C. No, I didn't do it.

    D. Yes, I'll consider it.

    * ever〔'ɛvɚ〕*adv.* 曾經　　consider〔kən'sɪdɚ〕*v.* 考慮
      move〔muv〕*v.* 搬家
      suburbs〔'sʌbɝbz〕*n. pl.* 郊區　　far〔far〕*adj.* 遠的

Part C

31. (**C**) M: What did you think of the play last night?

W: I enjoyed it, but I didn't have a very good seat.

M: That's a shame. But it is very popular.

W: Yes. I was lucky to be able to go at all.

Question : What is the woman's opinion?

A. The play wasn't very good.

B. The theater was too crowded.

C. The play is worth seeing.

D. The man was lucky to have a good seat.

* play〔ple〕n. 戲劇
  enjoy〔ɪn'dʒɔɪ〕v. 喜歡   seat〔sit〕n. 座位
  shame〔ʃem〕n. 可惜的事
  popular〔'pɑpjələ〕adj. 受歡迎的
  lucky〔'lʌkɪ〕adj. 幸運的
  be able to V. 能夠～   *at all* 竟然
  opinion〔ə'pɪnjən〕n. 意見
  theater〔'θiətə〕n. 劇場；戲院
  crowded〔'kraudɪd〕adj. 擁擠的
  worth〔wɜθ〕adj. 值得的

32. (**D**) W: Be careful where you put that knife. It's very sharp.

M: Don't worry. I haven't cut myself yet.

W: You're not the one I'm worried about. I don't
want the children to get hold of it.

Question : What did the man do?

A. He cut himself.

B. He played with a sharp knife.

C. He held a sharp knife near some children.

D. He put a knife where children could get it.

* careful〔'kɛrfəl〕adj. 小心的；謹慎的
  knife〔naɪf〕n. 刀子　　sharp〔ʃɑrp〕adj. 銳利的
  cut〔kʌt〕v. 切；割　　*not…yet* 尚未
  be worried about 擔心　　*get hold of* 拿到
  play with 玩　　near〔nɪr〕prep. 在…附近

33. (**B**) M : Do you know the name of this band?

W : No. I've never heard this before.

M : You're kidding! This song has been playing everywhere!

Question : What are they listening to?

A. An anonymous band.　　B. A popular song.

C. A new band.　　D. A new play.

* name〔nem〕n. 名稱　　band〔bænd〕n. 樂團
  kid〔kɪd〕v. 開玩笑
  You're kidding! 別開玩笑了！
  song〔sɔŋ〕n. 歌曲
  play〔ple〕v.（唱片）播放　n. 戲劇
  everywhere〔'ɛvrɪˌhwɛr〕adv. 到處　　*listen to* 聽
  anonymous〔ə'nɑnəməs〕adj. 不具名的；匿名的
  popular〔'pɑpjələ〕adj. 流行的；熱門的

34. (**C**) W: You've been playing computer games for a long
               time.

            M: It hasn't been that long.

            W: It's been over three hours. Don't you think you
               should start studying?

            M: If you say so.

            Question : What will the boy do?

            A. Play games for three hours.

            B. Say that he should study now.

            C. Begin to study now.

            D. Study for a long time.

            * computer〔kəm'pjutɚ〕 *n.* 電腦
              game〔gem〕 *n.* 遊戲
              over〔'ovɚ〕 *prep.* 超過
              start〔stɑrt〕 *v.* 開始   study〔'stʌdɪ〕 *v.* 讀書
              If you say so. 你說了算。   begin〔bɪ'gɪn〕 *v.* 開始

35. (**A**) M: Would you ever consider moving to the
               countryside?

            W: Oh, no. It's much too quiet for me.

            M: But that's the best part. No honking horns or
               noisy neighbors.

            W: No. I mean there's not much to do there.

            Question : Why does the man like the country?

            A. It is not noisy.

            B. There is not much to do.

C. Yes, he likes it very much.

D. It's the best part of the city.

* consider〔kən'sɪdə〕v. 考慮　　move〔muv〕v. 搬家
countryside〔'kʌntrɪˌsaɪd〕n. 鄉下　　*much too* 太；非常
quiet〔'kwaɪət〕adj. 安靜的　　part〔part〕n. 部份
honk〔hɔŋk〕v. 按（喇叭）　　horn〔hɔrn〕n. 喇叭
noisy〔'nɔɪzɪ〕adj. 吵鬧的　　neighbor〔'nebə〕n. 鄰居
mean〔min〕v. 意思是　　country〔'kʌntrɪ〕n. 鄉下

36.(**D**) W: The parking lot looks full.

M: Don't worry. They have valet parking. Just drive
up to the door, and they'll take care of it.

W: How much does it cost?

M: It's complimentary.

Question : What should the woman do?

A. Accept the compliment.

B. Drop the man off at the door.

C. Pay the valet a compliment.

D. Let the staff park her car.

* *parking lot* 停車場　　look〔luk〕v. 看起來
full〔ful〕adj. 滿的　　valet〔'vælɪt〕n.（旅館等的）服務生
valet parking 代客泊車　　*up to* 直到；達到
take care of 處理　　cost〔kɔst〕v. 需要（…錢）
complimentary〔ˌkɑmplə'mɛntərɪ〕adj. 免費的
accept〔ək'sɛpt〕v. 接受
compliment〔'kɑmpləmənt〕n. 稱讚
drop sb. off 下車　　pay〔pe〕v. 給予
staff〔stæf〕n. 工作人員　　park〔pɑrk〕v. 停（車）

37. (**C**) M: How are your knitting classes going?

W: Very slowly. I'm still working on the same sweater.

M: Relax. It'll get easier.

W: But I had planned to make everyone one for Christmas.

Question : What does the woman want to do?

A. Make the same sweater as the man.

B. Make everyone knit a sweater.

C. Give everyone a sweater for Christmas.

D. Get a job making sweaters.

* **How's ~ going?** ～進行得如何？　knit〔nɪt〕v. 編織
class〔klæs〕n. 課程　　slowly〔'slolɪ〕adv. 緩慢地
still〔stɪl〕adv. 仍然　　**work on** 致力於
the same 相同的　　sweater〔'swɛtɚ〕n. 毛衣
relax〔rɪ'læks〕v. 放輕鬆　　plan〔plæn〕v. 計畫
Christmas〔'krɪsməs〕n. 聖誕節
make〔mek〕v. 使

38. (**B**) W: It's hot in here. Is the AC on?

M: It's out of order.

W: Oh, no! Did you call the repairman?

M: Yes, but they can't send anyone out until tomorrow.

Question : What is the problem?

A. The weather is unusually warm.

B. The air conditioner is broken.

C. The repairman sent the wrong AC.

D. The man forgot to order an AC.

* **AC** 冷氣機 (= *air conditioner*)　　on〔ɑn〕*adv.* 開著的
out of order 故障　repairman〔rɪˈpɛrˌmæn〕*n.* 修理工人
send〔sɛnd〕*v.* 派　　**not…until~** 直到~才…
problem〔ˈprɑbləm〕*n.* 問題　　weather〔ˈwɛðɚ〕*n.* 天氣
unusually〔ʌnˈjuʒʊəlɪ〕*adv.* 異常地
warm〔wɔrm〕*adj.* 溫暖的　　*air conditioner* 冷氣機
broken〔ˈbrokən〕*adj.* 故障的
wrong〔rɔŋ〕*adj.* 錯誤的　　order〔ˈɔrdɚ〕*v.* 訂購

39. (**B**)　M: Wow. You have a lot of luggage. Why do you
　　　　　　need so much stuff for only two days?

　　　　W: It's not all for me. A lot of it is gifts for my sister
　　　　　　and her family.

　　　　M: Oh, are they going to be at the resort?

　　　　W: Yes. They're meeting us there.

　　Question : What does the woman have?

　A. She has to meet her sister at the resort.

　B. She has presents for her sister.

　C. She must carry everything herself.

　D. She has gifts for her parents and sister.

* wow〔waʊ〕*interj.* 哇；啊　　**a lot of** 很多的
luggage〔ˈlʌgɪdʒ〕*n.* 行李　　stuff〔stʌf〕*n.* 東西
gift〔gɪft〕*n.* 禮物　　family〔ˈfæməlɪ〕*n.* 家人
resort〔rɪˈzɔrt〕*n.* 渡假勝地　　meet〔mit〕*v.* 和…碰面
present〔ˈprɛznt〕*n.* 禮物 (= *gift*)
carry〔ˈkærɪ〕*v.* 提；拿　　parents〔ˈpɛrənts〕*n. pl.* 父母

40. (**C**) W: Aren't you taking a vacation this summer?

M: No, I'm taking time off in January.

W: Ah. You want to escape the cold, huh?

M: No, I'm going on a skiing holiday.

Question : Where will the man go on his vacation?

A. In the winter.　　　　B. To a warm place.

C. To a ski resort.　　　　D. Later in the year.

* vacation〔veˋkeʃən〕*n.* 假期　***take a vacation*** 休假
take time off 休假　January〔ˋdʒænjʊˏɛrɪ〕*n.* 一月
ah〔ɑ〕*interj.* 哈；啊　escape〔əˋskep〕*v.* 躲避
cold〔kold〕*n.* 寒冷　huh〔hʌ〕*interj.* 哈；什麼？
skiing〔ˋskiɪŋ〕*n.* 滑雪
holiday〔ˋhɑləˏde〕*n.* 節日；假日　ski〔ski〕*adj.* 滑雪的
a ski resort 滑雪勝地　later〔ˋletɚ〕*adv.* 後來

41. (**B**) M: Be careful. You're not supposed to cross the
street here.

W: But there's hardly any traffic.

M: Yes, but you could get a ticket. There's a police
officer right over there.

W: Oh, thanks. I'll use the crosswalk.

Question : What kind of ticket could the woman get?

A. A traffic ticket.

B. A jaywalking ticket.

C. A parking ticket.

D. A speeding ticket.

* **be supposed to V.** 應該～　　cross〔krɔs〕v. 橫越
  street〔strit〕n. 街道　　hardly〔'hardlɪ〕adv. 幾乎不
  there's hardly 幾乎沒有
  traffic〔'træfɪk〕n. 交通；交通流量
  ticket〔'tɪkɪt〕n. 罰單　　officer〔'ɔfəsɚ〕n. 警官
  police officer 警員　　**right over there** 就在那裡
  crosswalk〔'krɔs,wɔk〕n. 行人穿越道
  traffic ticket 交通違規罰單
  jaywalk〔'dʒe,wɔk〕v. 擅自穿越馬路
  jaywalking ticket 行人擅自穿越馬路罰單
  park〔park〕v. 停車　　**parking ticket** 違規停車罰單
  speeding〔'spidɪŋ〕adj. 超速的
  speeding ticket 汽車超速罰單

42. (**D**)　W: Hey, I've been calling you.　Didn't you hear me?
　　　　　　M: Sorry.　I guess I've got my music up too loud.
　　　　　　W: You shouldn't do that.　You could damage your
　　　　　　　　hearing with those things.

　　　　　Question : What things is the woman talking about?

　　　　　A. songs.　　　　　　B. radios.
　　　　　C. volumes.　　　　　D. earphones.

* hey〔he〕interj. 嘿　　call〔kɔl〕v. 叫
  guess〔gɛs〕v. 猜　　music〔'mjuzɪk〕n. 音樂
  loud〔laud〕adj. 大聲的
  get one's **music up too loud** 把音樂開得太大聲
  damage〔'dæmɪdʒ〕v. 損害　　hearing〔'hɪrɪŋ〕n. 聽力
  talk about 談論　　radio〔'redɪ,o〕n. 收音機
  volume〔'valjəm〕n. (大型) 書本【如作「音量」解時，則是
  　不可數名詞，字尾不可加 s】　　earphone〔'ɪr,fon〕n. 耳機

43. (**B**) M: Wow. It's bright today.

W: You'd better put on your sunglasses.

M: I can't. I've misplaced them.

W: Again? Isn't that the second pair this week?

Question : What did the man do?

A. He placed his sunglasses on his face.

B. He lost two pairs of sunglasses.

C. He broke his sunglasses.

D. He missed the sunglasses twice this week.

* bright〔braɪt〕adj. 晴朗的
  had better 最好　　***put on*** 戴上
  sunglasses〔'sʌn͵glæsɪz〕n. pl. 太陽眼鏡
  misplace〔mɪs'ples〕v. 誤放　***Again?*** 又來了？
  second〔'sɛkənd〕adj. 第二的
  pair〔pɛr〕n. 一副　　place〔ples〕v. 放置
  face〔fes〕n. 臉部　　lose〔luz〕v. 遺失
  break〔brek〕v. 打破
  miss〔mɪs〕v. 發覺⋯不見了
  twice〔twaɪs〕adv. 兩次

44. (**D**) W: How many in your party, sir?

M: Just myself.

W: Very well. I have a nice table by the window, but it's in nonsmoking.

M: That will be fine.

Question : What can't the man do?

A. Sit by himself.   B. Have a party.

C. Sit by the window.   D. Smoke in the restaurant.

* party (ˈpɑrtɪ) n. 一行人   sir (sɝ , sə) n. 先生
Very well. 好。   nice (naɪs) adj. 不錯的
by (baɪ) prep. 在…旁邊   window (ˈwɪndo) n. 窗戶
nonsmoking (ˈnɑnˈsmokɪŋ) adj. 禁煙的
by oneself 獨自地   **have a party** 舉辦宴會
smoke (smok) v. 抽煙   restaurant (ˈrɛstərənt) n. 餐廳

45. (**A**) M : Good morning. I'd like to get some information
            about French classes.

   W : We offer three levels of classes starting every
            Monday. But I'm afraid the advanced class is full.

   M : Oh, I'm a beginner.

   W : In that case, you can begin next week.

   Question : When will the man start French classes?

   A. Next Monday.   B. He cannot.

   C. On the weekend.   D. Every Monday.

* **would like to V.** 想要～
information (ˌɪnfəˈmeʃən) n. 資訊
French (frɛntʃ) adj. 法語的   class (klæs) n. 課程
offer (ˈɔfə) v. 提供   level (ˈlɛvl̩) n. 程度；等級
start (start) v. 開始   **I'm afraid～** 恐怕
advanced (ədˈvænst) adj. 進階的；高級的
full (ful) adj. 滿的   beginner (bɪˈgɪnə) n. 初學者
case (kes) n. 情況   **in that case** 那樣的話
begin (bɪˈgɪn) v. 開始   weekend (ˈwikˈɛnd) n. 週末

English Listening Comprehension Test
Test Book No. 7

This listening comprehension test will test your ability to understand spoken English. In this test, each conversation, statement and question will be spoken JUST ONE TIME. They will not be written out for you. There are three parts to this test. Special instructions will be given to you at the beginning of each part.

Part A

In Part A, you will see several pictures in your test book. For each picture, you will be asked 1 to 3 questions. For each question, you will hear four possible answers. Choose the best answer according to what you see in the picture.

Example:

<u>You will see</u>:

<u>You will hear</u>: What is this?
   A. This is a table.
   B. This is a chair.
   C. This is a watch.
   D. This is a doll.

The best answer to the question "What is this?" is B: "This is a chair." Therefore, you should choose answer B.

A. **Questions 1-3**

B. **Questions 4-6**

C. <u>Questions 7-9</u>

D. <u>Questions 10-11</u>

E. <u>Questions 12-13</u>

F. <u>Questions 14-15</u>

Part B

In Part B, you will hear 15 questions. After you hear a question, read the four possible answers in your test book and decide which one is the best answer to the question you have heard.

Example:

<u>You will hear</u>: What does your father do?

<u>You will read</u>: A. He's 50 years old.
B. He's a teacher.
C. He's hungry.
D. He's in Los Angeles.

The best answer to the question "What does your father do?" is B: "He's a teacher." Therefore, you should choose answer B.

16. A. Yes, I do.
B. I've got about 15 minutes.
C. It's half past four.
D. It's a Rolex.

17. A. Yes. They're still in the door.
B. Yes, I saw you do it.
C. I put them on the table.
D. Just turn it to the right.

18. A. I'm looking forward to it, too.
   B. Because I have to work late.
   C. I'll bring some pizza.
   D. About seven-thirty.

19. A. Thanks.
   B. You shouldn't have.
   C. You're welcome.
   D. I owe you one.

20. A. She's a humorous person.
   B. She enjoys listening to music.
   C. Yes, I like her very much.
   D. She looks just like her mother.

21. A. Yes. Here's your share.
   B. I wouldn't miss it.
   C. No, I'll be there.
   D. Let's take a taxi.

22. A. He's from Tainan.
   B. No. Let's invite him over.
   C. Yes, I can drive him.
   D. When will you arrive?

23. A. Actually, it's a bit too sweet.
   B. Indeed, it's fatty.
   C. I like cake.
   D. This isn't, either.

24. A. Hello, Diane.
   B. I'll stop by around six.
   C. I won't.
   D. Sure, I did.

25. A. I got it at Sogo.
    B. I used my credit card.
    C. This change is not right.
    D. It was five hundred.

26. A. Congratulations. You deserve it.
    B. Is he the tall man over there?
    C. We'll find one soon.
    D. I don't think it's open yet.

27. A. How many pills should I take?
    B. Could you take a message?
    C. Thanks, but I don't need one.
    D. I'll pay it next week.

28. A. He was caught cheating.
    B. It was my turn.
    C. I missed too many classes.
    D. He's nothing special.

29. A. Yes, I've made it many times.
    B. No, I didn't.
    C. It's really not that hard.
    D. I'll have another order.

30. A. I'm leaving from Taiwan Taoyuan International Airport.
    B. I prefer to fly business class.
    C. I'm going with China Airlines.
    D. It leaves from gate 12.

Part C

In Part C, you will hear 15 conversations between a man and a woman. After each conversation, you will hear a question about the conversation. After you hear the question, read the four possible answers in your test book and choose the best answer to the question you have heard.

Example:

You will hear: (Man)　　How do you go to school every day?

(Woman)　Usually by bus. Sometimes by taxi.

Question: How does the woman go to school?

You will read:　A. She always goes to school on foot.

B. She usually rides a bike.

C. She takes either a bus or a taxi.

D. She usually goes to school by bus, never by taxi.

The best answer to the question "How does the woman go to school?" is C: "She takes either a bus or a taxi." Therefore, you should choose answer C.

31. A. Writing in her book.
    B. Borrowing his book.
    C. Placing markers in her book.
    D. Referring to a paper.

32. A. Take shelter in the shop until the rain stops.
    B. Buy two umbrellas.
    C. Get a drink in the store.
    D. Share their umbrella.

33. A. A novel.
    B. A chalkboard.
    C. A restaurant.
    D. A menu.

34. A. You can pay a flat fee.
    B. You get two free rides.
    C. You have to pay all the money first.
    D. You can go to the museum.

35. A. He wants to amend his order.
    B. He wants to talk to the woman.
    C. He wants to cancel his order.
    D. He wants his order as soon as possible.

36. A. Camping.
    B. Telling ghost stories.
    C. Drinking the water.
    D. Lighting fires.

37. A. It's in the lobby.
    B. They should take the stairs to the roof.
    C. They should take an elevator from the lobby.
    D. They cannot go to the pool unless it's an emergency.

38. A. She does not have enough supplies for the holiday.
    B. She did not get a three-day weekend.
    C. She cannot find affordable transportation.
    D. She is too demanding.

39. A. He wants the woman to
    take care of his garden.
    B. He wants to have
    beautiful flowerbeds.
    C. He wants the boy to
    cut his grass.
    D. He wants to look at the
    woman's lawn.

40. A. His son often cries at
    night.
    B. His neighbor has a new
    baby.
    C. He is babysitting a little
    boy.
    D. His neighbor is too
    noisy.

41. A. A salad and a dish of
    dressing.
    B. A vinegar salad.
    C. A soup and salad.
    D. Soup and a side salad.

42. A. An action film.
    B. A ghost story.
    C. A violent movie.
    D. A cartoon.

43. A. He ran ten kilometers
    that morning.
    B. He went running with
    his wife.
    C. He competed in a
    ten-kilometer race.
    D. He won a marathon.

44. A. She bought it at a
    famous store.
    B. She received it as a gift.
    C. She designed it herself.
    D. She made it.

45. A. An art museum.
    B. An animal exhibition.
    C. An impressionist show.
    D. A natural history
    museum.

Listening Test 7 詳解

Part A

For questions number 1 to 3, please look at picture A.

1. (**B**) Who is on the stage?
   A. A computer.
   B. A model.
   C. A photographer.
   D. A salesman.

   * stage (stedʒ) *n.* 舞台
     computer (kəm'pjutə) *n.* 電腦
     model ('modl̩) *n.* 模特兒
     photographer (fə'tɑgrəfə) *n.* 攝影師
     salesman ('selzmən) *n.* 推銷員；售貨員

2. (**A**) Please look at picture A again. What is the woman wearing?
   A. Shorts.
   B. A mini-skirt.
   C. Boots.
   D. A calculator.

   * wear (wɛr) *v.* 穿；戴
     shorts (ʃɔrts) *n. pl.* 短褲
     mini-skirt 迷你裙   boot (but) *n.* 靴子
     calculator ('kælkjə,letə) *n.* 計算機

3. (**C**) Please look at picture A again. What are the men doing?

     A. They are photographs.

     B. They are selling cameras.

     C. They are taking pictures.

     D. They are getting autographs.

     * photograph〔'fotə,græf〕*n.* 照片　　sell〔sɛl〕*v.* 賣

     camera〔'kæmərə〕*n.* 照相機　　picture〔'pɪktʃə〕*n.* 照片

     take pictures 拍照　　autograph〔'ɔtə,græf〕*n.* 親筆簽名

For questions number 4 to 6, please look at picture B.

4. (**C**) What are the girl and dog wearing?

     A. A leash.　　　　　　B. An umbrella.

     C. Hoods.　　　　　　 D. UVs.

     * leash〔liʃ〕*n.*（拴狗用的）鍊子；皮帶

     umbrella〔ʌm'brɛlə〕*n.* 雨傘

     hood〔hʊd〕*n.* 頭巾；兜帽；頭罩

     UV 紫外線（= *ultraviolet*）

5. (**D**) Please look at picture B again. What does the girl on the right think?

     A. She has an umbrella.　　B. Afraid.

     C. She is satisfied.

     D. The other girl is odd.

     * right〔raɪt〕*n.* 右邊　　afraid〔ə'fred〕*adj.* 害怕的

     satisfied〔'sætɪs,faɪd〕*adj.* 滿足的；滿意的

     the other 另一個　　odd〔ɑd〕*adj.* 古怪的

6. (**B**) Please look at picture B again.　What are they doing?

      A. It is Halloween.　　　　B. Taking a walk.

      C. Trick or treating.　　　　D. They are sisters.

      * Halloween〔͵hælo'in〕*n.* 萬聖節前夕（即十月三十一日晚上）

      take a walk 散步

      trick or treat 不給糖就搗蛋【指萬聖節孩子們挨家逐戶要糖

      果等禮物，如不遂願便惡作劇一番的習俗】

For questions number 7 to 9, please look at picture C.

7. (**D**) What is the boy rabbit doing?

      A. Winking.　　　　　　B. On a computer.

      C. Taking a picture.　　　　D. Typing.

      * boy〔bɔɪ〕*adj.* 男孩的；年少的

      rabbit〔'ræbɪt〕*n.* 兔子

      wink〔wɪŋk〕*v.* 眨眼　　type〔taɪp〕*v.* 打字

8. (**B**) Please look at picture C again.　What is he thinking?

      A. With one eye.　　　　B. About a girl.

      C. Coffee.　　　　　　　D. He isn't drinking.

      * coffee〔'kɔfɪ〕*n.* 咖啡　　drink〔drɪŋk〕*v.* 喝

9. (**D**) Please look at picture C again.　What is in his hand?

      A. A computer.　　　　B. Love.

      C. A picture.　　　　　D. A mouse.

      * love〔lʌv〕*n.* 愛　　mouse〔maʊs〕*n.* 滑鼠

For questions number 10 and 11, please look at picture D.

10. (**D**) What is the boy's problem?
    A. He is swimming.   B. He is thirsty.
    C. He is lost.   D. He is drowning.

    * problem ('prɑbləm) *n.* 問題   swim (swɪm) *v.* 游泳
    thirsty ('θɝstɪ) *adj.* 口渴的   lost (lɔst) *adj.* 迷路的
    drown (draʊn) *v.* 溺死;淹死

11. (**B**) Please look at picture D again. What is he doing?
    A. Splashing.   B. Waving.
    C. Floating.   D. Falling.

    * splash (splæʃ) *v.* 潑水;使水濺起
    wave (wev) *v.* 揮手
    float (flot) *v.* 飄浮;漂浮   fall (fɔl) *v.* 落下

For questions number 12 and 13, please look at picture E.

12. (**B**) Who is the boy?
    A. He is riding a bicycle.
    B. He is a mail carrier.
    C. He is happy.
    D. He is careless.

    * ride (raɪd) *v.* 騎   bicycle ('baɪsɪkl̩) *n.* 腳踏車
    mail (mel) *n.* 信件   carrier ('kærɪɚ) *n.* 運送人
    mail carrier 郵差 (= *mailman* = *postman*)
    careless ('kɛrlɪs) *adj.* 不小心的;粗心的

13. (**D**)　Please look at picture E again.　What is the girl doing?

    A.　She is mailing a letter.

    B.　She is a customer.

    C.　She is chasing the thief.

    D.　She is catching the letters.

    * mail〔mel〕v. 郵寄　　letter〔'lɛtɚ〕n. 信

    customer〔'kʌstəmɚ〕n. 顧客　　chase〔tʃes〕v. 追趕

    thief〔θif〕n. 小偷　　catch〔kætʃ〕v. 接

For questions number 14 and 15, please look at picture F.

14. (**C**)　Who is being carried?

    A.　The boy on the bike.　　B.　The boy in the middle.

    C.　The baby.　　　　　　　D.　The girl.

    * carry〔'kærɪ〕v. 抱；揹

    bike〔baɪk〕n. 腳踏車；摩托車

    middle〔'mɪdḷ〕n. 中間　　baby〔'bebɪ〕n. 嬰兒

15. (**D**)　Please look at picture F again.　What is the unhappy

    boy doing?

    A.　Screaming.　　　　　　B.　Laughing.

    C.　Jumping rope.　　　　　D.　Babysitting.

    * unhappy〔ʌn'hæpɪ〕adj. 不愉快的

    scream〔skrim〕v. 尖叫　　laugh〔læf〕v. 笑

    jump〔dʒʌmp〕v. 跳　　rope〔rop〕n. 繩子

    jump rope 跳繩

    babysit〔'bebɪˌsɪt〕v. 照顧嬰兒；擔任褓姆

Part B

16. (**C**)　What time do you have now?

      A.　Yes, I do.　　　　　B.　I've got about 15 minutes.

      C.　It's half past four.　　D.　It's a Rolex.

> * **What time do you have?** 現在幾點？
> **I've got** 我有（= I have）　　minute ('mɪnɪt) *n.* 分鐘
> half (hæf) *n.* 一半　　past (pæst) *prep.* 過了
> **half past four** 四點半
> Rolex ('rolɛks) *n.* 勞力士【手錶品牌】

17. (**A**)　Did you see where I put my keys?

      A.　Yes.　They're still in the door.

      B.　Yes, I saw you do it.

      C.　I put them on the table.

      D.　Just turn it to the right.

> * put (pʊt) *v.* 放　　key (ki) *n.* 鑰匙
> still (stɪl) *adv.* 仍然　　turn (tɜn) *v.* 轉
> right (raɪt) *n.* 右邊

18. (**D**)　When should I expect you home?

      A.　I'm looking forward to it, too.

      B.　Because I have to work late.

      C.　I'll bring some pizza.

      D.　About seven-thirty.

> * expect (ɪk'spɛkt) *v.* 預期；期待　　**look forward to** 期待
> late (let) *adv.* 晚；遲　　bring (brɪŋ) *v.* 帶來
> pizza ('pitsə) *n.* 披薩

19. (**A**) Here's the pen I borrowed yesterday.

    A. Thanks.   B. You shouldn't have.

    C. You're welcome.   D. I owe you one.

    * borrow ('baro) v. 借 (出)

    You're welcome. 不客氣。   owe (o) v. 欠

    I owe you one. 我欠你一次；我欠你一份人情。

20. (**B**) What does Kathy like to do?

    A. She's a humorous person.

    B. She enjoys listening to music.

    C. Yes, I like her very much.

    D. She looks just like her mother.

    * like (laɪk) v. 喜歡

    humorous ('hjumərəs) adj. 幽默的

    enjoy (ɪn'dʒɔɪ) v. 喜歡   music ('mjuzɪk) n. 音樂

    look like 看起來像

21. (**B**) You're going to the party, aren't you?

    A. Yes. Here's your share.

    B. I wouldn't miss it.

    C. No, I'll be there.

    D. Let's take a taxi.

    * party ('partɪ) n. 宴會

    share (ʃɛr) n. (一人持有的) 份；部份

    your share 你應得的一份   miss (mɪs) v. 錯過

    take (tek) v. 搭乘   taxi ('tæksɪ) n. 計程車

22. (**B**) Did you know that Jack is in town?

    A. He's from Tainan.

    B. No. Let's invite him over.

    C. Yes, I can drive him.

    D. When will you arrive?

    * town〔taʊn〕n. 城；鎮　*in town* 在城裡
    Tainan 台南　invite〔ɪn'vaɪt〕v. 邀請
    invite sb. over 邀請某人來家中作客
    drive〔draɪv〕v. 開車載（某人）
    arrive〔ə'raɪv〕v. 到達

23. (**A**) Isn't this cake delicious?

    A. Actually, it's a bit too sweet.

    B. Indeed, it's fatty.

    C. I like cake.

    D. This isn't, either.

    * cake〔kek〕n. 蛋糕　delicious〔dɪ'lɪʃəs〕adj. 美味的
    actually〔'æktʃʊəlɪ〕adv. 其實；實際上
    a bit 有點　sweet〔swit〕adj. 甜的
    indeed〔ɪn'did〕adv. 的確　fatty〔'fætɪ〕adj. 油膩的
    either〔'iðɚ〕adv. 也（不）【用於否定句】

24. (**C**) Don't forget to call Diane tonight.

    A. Hello, Diane.　 B. I'll stop by around six.

    C. I won't.　 D. Sure, I did.

    * forget〔fɚ'gɛt〕v. 忘記　call〔kɔl〕v. 打電話給
    Diane〔daɪ'æn〕n. 黛安　*stop by* 順道拜訪
    around〔ə'raʊnd〕adv. 大約

25. (**D**) How much did you pay for that bag?
    A. I got it at Sogo.   B. I used my credit card.
    C. This change is not right.   D. It was five hundred.

    * pay〔pe〕v. 付（錢）< *for* >   bag〔bæg〕n. 包包
    get〔gɛt〕v. 買   credit〔'krɛdɪt〕n. 信用
    credit card 信用卡   change〔tʃendʒ〕n. 零錢；找的錢
    right〔raɪt〕adj. 正確的

26. (**B**) Have you seen the new store manager?
    A. Congratulations. You deserve it.
    B. Is he the tall man over there?
    C. We'll find one soon.
    D. I don't think it's open yet.

    * store〔stor〕n. 商店   manager〔'mænɪdʒɚ〕n. 經理
    congratulations〔kən,grætʃə'leʃənz〕n. pl. 恭喜
    deserve〔dɪ'zɝv〕v. 應得   tall〔tɔl〕adj. 高的
    over there 在那裡   find〔faɪnd〕v. 找到
    soon〔sun〕adv. 很快   open〔'opən〕v.（商店）開張
    I don't think it's open yet. 我不認爲那家店開了；我認爲
    那家店還沒開。(= *I think it's not open yet.*)

27. (**B**) There's a call for you.
    A. How many pills should I take?
    B. Could you take a message?
    C. Thanks, but I don't need one.
    D. I'll pay it next week.

    * call〔kɔl〕n.（一通）電話   pill〔pɪl〕n. 藥丸
    take〔tek〕v. 服用   message〔'mɛsɪdʒ〕n. 訊息
    take a message 記錄留言   need〔nid〕v. 需要

28. (**C**) Why did Mr. Robertson flunk you?

A. He was caught cheating.

B. It was my turn.

C. I missed too many classes.

D. He's nothing special.

* Mr. (ˈmɪstə) n. …先生

Robertson (ˈrɑbɜsn̩) n. 羅伯森

flunk (flʌŋk) v. 使…不及格

catch (kætʃ) v. 抓到；當場撞見

cheat (tʃit) v. 作弊　　turn (tɜn) n. 輪流順序

It was my turn. 輪到我了。　　miss (mɪs) v. 缺（課）

special (ˈspɛʃəl) adj. 特別的

29. (**C**) How ever did you make this wonderful soup?

A. Yes, I've made it many times.

B. No, I didn't.

C. It's really not that hard.

D. I'll have another order.

* ever (ˈɛvə) adv. 究竟；到底

wonderful (ˈwʌndəfəl) adj. 很棒的

soup (sup) n. 湯　　time (taɪm) n. 次數

really (ˈriəlɪ) adv. 眞地

hard (hɑrd) adj. 困難的　　have (hæv) v. 吃

another (əˈnʌðə) adj. 另一個

order (ˈɔrdə) n. （菜、餐點的）一份

30. (**C**) Which airline are you taking?

    A. I'm leaving from Taiwan Taoyuan International Airport.

    B. I prefer to fly business class.

    C. I'm going with China Airlines.

    D. It leaves from gate 12.

    * airline ('ɛr,laɪn) *n.* 航空公司
       take (tek) *v.* 搭乘   leave (liv) *v.* 離開
       Taiwan ('taɪ'wɑn) *n.* 台灣
       international (,ɪntə'næʃənḷ) *adj.* 國際的
       airport ('ɛr,port) *n.* 機場
       Taiwan Taoyuan International Airport 台灣桃園國際機場
       prefer (prɪ'fɝ) *v.* 比較喜歡
       fly (flaɪ) *v.* 搭（飛機）
       business ('bɪznɪs) *n.* 商業   ***business class*** 商務艙
       China Airlines 中華航空公司   gate (get) *n.* 登機門

Part C

31. (**C**) M : Can I take a look at your book?

    W : Sure. Just don't remove any of the bookmarks, please.

    M : What are they for?

    W : I've been marking passages I may refer to in my paper.

    Question : What has the woman been doing?

A. Writing in her book.　　B. Borrowing his book.

C. Placing markers in her book.

D. Referring to a paper.

* ***take a look at*** 看一看　　remove〔rɪ'muv〕*v.* 移動；除去
  bookmark〔'bʊk͵mɑrk〕*n.* 書籤
  mark〔mɑrk〕*v.* 在⋯做記號
  passage〔'pæsɪdʒ〕*n.* (一段)文章
  refer〔rɪ'fɜ〕*v.* 參考；引用；提到 < *to* >
  paper〔'pepɚ〕*n.* 報告　　borrow〔'bɑro〕*v.* 借(入)
  place〔ples〕*v.* 放置　　marker〔'mɑrkɚ〕*n.* 標籤；標記

32. (**B**)　W: It's starting to rain. Do you have an umbrella?

　　　　 M: No, I left it at the office.

　　　　 W: I don't have one, either. Let's run into this
　　　　　　 convenience store and get a couple.

　　 Question : What will they do?

A. Take shelter in the shop until the rain stops.

B. Buy two umbrellas.　　C. Get a drink in the store.

D. Share their umbrella.

* start〔stɑrt〕*v.* 開始　　rain〔ren〕*v.* 下雨
  umbrella〔ʌm'brɛlə〕*n.* 雨傘
  leave〔liv〕*v.* 遺留；忘記帶走　　office〔'ɔfɪs〕*n.* 辦公室
  either〔'iðɚ〕*adv.* 也(不)【用於否定句】
  convenience〔kən'vinjəns〕*n.* 方便；便利
  convenience store 便利商店　　get〔gɛt〕*v.* 買
  couple〔'kʌpl̩〕*n.* 一對；兩個　　shelter〔'ʃɛltɚ〕*n.* 遮蔽物
  take shelter 躲雨　　until〔ən'tɪl〕*prep.* 直到
  stop〔stɑp〕*v.* 停止　　drink〔drɪŋk〕*n.* 飲料
  share〔ʃɛr〕*v.* 共用；分享

33. (**D**) M : Do you have any specials today?

W : Yes. If you order one of the lunch specials on page two, you get a second one for half price.

M : I don't see that. Can you show me where?

W : You've passed it. Turn back one page.

Question : What are they looking at?

A. A novel.

B. A chalkboard.

C. A restaurant.

D. A menu.

* special (ˈspɛʃəl) n. 特餐　　order (ˈɔrdɚ) v. 點 (餐)
page (pedʒ) n. 頁　　second (ˈsɛkənd) adj. 第二的
half (hæf) adj. 一半的　　price (praɪs) n. 價格
show (ʃo) v. 指給…看　　pass (pæs) v. 超過
turn (tɝn) v. 翻 (頁)　　back (bæk) adv. 向後
look at 看　　novel (ˈnɑvl) n. 小說
chalkboard (ˈtʃɔk‚bɔrd) n. 黑板 (= *blackboard*)
restaurant (ˈrɛstərənt) n. 餐廳
menu (ˈmɛnju) n. 菜單

34. (**B**) W : How much is the fare to the museum?

M : All city buses charge a flat fee of one dollar, but it's cheaper if you buy a bus pass.

W : How does that work?

M : You pay ten dollars up front, and you get twelve rides.

Question : What is the advantage of buying a bus pass?

A. You can pay a flat fee.

B. You get two free rides.

C. You have to pay all the money first.

D. You can go to the museum.

* fare〔fɛr〕*n.* 車資

museum〔mju'ziəm〕*n.* 博物館

city bus 市區公車　　　charge〔tʃɑrdʒ〕*v.* 收費

flat〔flæt〕*adj.* 均一的　　fee〔fi〕*n.* 費用

cheap〔tʃip〕*adj.* 便宜的　　pass〔pæs〕*n.* 通行證

bus pass 公車特價優惠票　　work〔wɜk〕*v.* 運作

up front 最前面；一開始　　ride〔raɪd〕*n.* 搭乘（次數）

advantage〔əd'væntɪdʒ〕*n.* 優點；好處

free〔fri〕*adj.* 免費的

first〔fɜst〕*adv.* 最先地；起初地

35. (**A**) M : Boss, Mr. Jones is on the phone. He's asking if you received his order.

W : Yes, we got it. Tell him it should go out this afternoon.

M : Now he says he wants to change it.

W : I'd better talk to him.

Question : What does Mr. Jones want?

A. He wants to amend his order.

B. He wants to talk to the woman.

C. He wants to cancel his order.

D. He wants his order as soon as possible.

* boss〔bɔs〕*n.* 老闆　　Mr.〔'mɪstɚ〕*n.* …先生
Jones〔dʒonz〕*n.* 瓊斯
phone〔fon〕*n.* 電話（= telephone）
on the phone 電話中；講電話　　if〔ɪf〕*conj.* 是否
receive〔rɪ'siv〕*v.* 收到　　order〔'ɔrdɚ〕*n.* 訂單；訂貨
go out 送出　　change〔tʃendʒ〕*v.* 更改
had better V. 最好~　　amend〔ə'mɛnd〕*v.* 修正；變更
cancel〔'kænsl̩〕*v.* 取消　　*as soon as possible* 儘快

36. (**D**)　W: I'm really looking forward to our camping trip.

M: Me, too.　Nothing beats sitting around the campfire telling ghost stories.

W: But we can't do that now.　It's not allowed in the dry season.

M: Oh, that's too bad.

Question : What is not allowed?

A. Camping.　　　　　　B. Telling ghost stories.

C. Drinking the water.　　D. Lighting fires.

* really〔'rɪəlɪ〕*adv.* 眞地　　*look forward to* 期待
camp〔kæmp〕*v.* 露營　　trip〔trɪp〕*n.* 旅行
camping trip 露營之旅　　beat〔bit〕*v.* 勝過
around〔ə'raʊnd〕*prep.* 圍著
campfire〔'kæmp,faɪr〕*n.* 營火　　ghost〔gost〕*n.* 鬼
story〔'storɪ〕*n.* 故事　　allow〔ə'laʊ〕*v.* 允許
dry〔draɪ〕*adj.* 乾燥的　　season〔'sizn̩〕*n.* 季節
bad〔bæd〕*adj.* 可惜的；糟糕的　　light〔laɪt〕*v.* 生（火）
fire〔faɪr〕*n.* 火　　*light a fire* 生火

37. (**C**)　M: Is it possible to get to the swimming pool this way?

　　　　W: No. You need to go back downstairs to the lobby and then take the elevator back up.

　　　　M: But aren't there any stairs up to the rooftop pool?

　　　　W: Yes, but they're for emergencies only.

　　　　Question : How should swimmers get to the pool?

　　　　A. It's in the lobby.

　　　　B. They should take the stairs to the roof.

　　　　C. They should take an elevator from the lobby.

　　　　D. They cannot go to the pool unless it's an emergency.

　　　* possible (ˈpɑsəbḷ) adj. 可能的　　***get to*** 到達
　　　pool (pul) n. 水池　　***swimming pool*** 游泳池
　　　way (we) n. 方向
　　　downstairs (ˈdaʊnˈstɛrz) adv. 到樓下
　　　lobby (ˈlɑbɪ) n. 大廳　　elevator (ˈɛlə͵vetə) n. 電梯
　　　back up 回到樓上　　stair (stɛr) n. 樓梯
　　　up to 上去　　rooftop (ˈruf͵tɑp) adj. 屋頂上的
　　　emergency (ɪˈmɝdʒənsɪ) n. 緊急情況
　　　swimmer (ˈswɪmə) n. 游泳者　　***take the stairs*** 走樓梯
　　　roof (ruf) n. 屋頂　　unless (ənˈlɛs) conj. 除非

38. (**C**)　W: I can't understand it. Why are the bus and train fares so high?

　　　　M: It's because of the long weekend coming. Supply and demand, you know.

　　　　W: Maybe I should just fly instead.

M：I wouldn't recommend that. Airfares have
　　doubled, too.

Question：What is the woman's problem?

A. She does not have enough supplies for the holiday.

B. She did not get a three-day weekend.

C. She cannot find affordable transportation.

D. She is too demanding.

* understand（͵ʌndɚ'stænd）v. 了解　　fare（fɛr）n. 車資
　high（haɪ）adj. 高的　　weekend（'wik'ɛnd）n. 週末
　long weekend 長週末【指週六、週日，再加上星期五或星期一】
　come（kʌm）v. 到來　　supply（sə'plaɪ）n. 供給
　demand（dɪ'mænd）n. 需求　　maybe（'mebi）adv. 或許
　fly（flaɪ）v. 搭飛機　　instead（ɪn'stɛd）adv. 作為代替
　recommend（͵rɛkə'mɛnd）v. 推薦；建議
　airfare（'ɛr͵fɛr）n. 飛機票價
　double（'dʌbl̩）v. 變成兩倍　　enough（ə'nʌf）adj. 足夠的
　supplies（sə'plaɪz）n. pl. 儲備物資
　holiday（'hɑlə͵de）n. 假日
　affordable（ə'fɔrdəbl̩）adj. 負擔得起的
　transportation（͵trænspɚ'teʃən）n. 運輸工具
　demanding（dɪ'mændɪŋ）adj. 要求過多的；苛求的

39.（ **C** ）M：Who takes care of your yard? It looks lovely.

　　W：One of the neighborhood boys mows the grass,
　　　　but I take care of the flowerbeds myself.

　　M：Could you give me his number? I'd love it if my
　　　　lawn looked this good.

Question : What does the man want?

A. He wants the woman to take care of his garden.

B. He wants to have beautiful flowerbeds.

C. He wants the boy to cut his grass.

D. He wants to look at the woman's lawn.

* **take care of** 照顧　　yard〔jɑrd〕n. 庭院
lovely〔'lʌvlɪ〕adj. 可愛的；美麗的
neighborhood〔'nebə͵hʊd〕adj. 附近的
mow〔mo〕v. 除（草）　　grass〔græs〕n. 草
flowerbed〔'flaʊə͵bɛd〕n. 花壇
number〔'nʌmbə〕n. 電話號碼　　lawn〔lɔn〕n. 草坪
this〔ðɪs〕adv. 這麼　　garden〔'gɑrdn̩〕n. 花園；庭院
cut〔kʌt〕v. 修剪（花草）

40. (**D**) W: You look awfully tired today.　Is the new baby keeping you up?

M: No.　He doesn't cry as much as I expected.　The real problem is our new neighbor.

W: What does he do?

M: He plays loud music most of the night.

Question : Why can't the man sleep?

A. His son often cries at night.

B. His neighbor has a new baby.

C. He is babysitting a little boy.

D. His neighbor is too noisy.

* awfully〔'ɔflɪ〕adv. 非常地   tired〔taɪrd〕adj. 疲倦的
  new baby 新生兒   up〔ʌp〕adj. 沒睡覺的
  as much as 和…一樣多   expect〔ɪk'spɛkt〕v. 預期
  real〔'rɪəl〕adj. 眞正的   problem〔'prɑbləm〕n. 問題
  neighbor〔'nebɚ〕n. 鄰居   play〔ple〕v. 播放
  loud〔laʊd〕adj. 大聲的   music〔'mjuzɪk〕n. 音樂
  most〔most〕pron. 大部份   sleep〔slip〕v. 睡
  son〔sʌn〕n. 兒子   often〔'ɔfən〕adv. 常常
  babysit〔'bebɪˌsɪt〕v. 照顧嬰兒；擔任褓姆
  little〔'lɪtḷ〕adj. 小的   noisy〔'nɔɪzɪ〕adj. 吵鬧的

41. (**A**) M: Would you prefer soup or salad?

W: A salad, please, with the dressing on the side.

M: No problem. We have French, blue cheese, or
  vinaigrette.

W: The vinaigrette.

Question : What did the woman order?

A. A salad and a dish of dressing.

B. A vinegar salad.   C. A soup and salad.

D. Soup and a side salad.

* prefer〔prɪ'fɝ〕v. 比較喜歡   soup〔sup〕n. 湯
  salad〔'sæləd〕n. 沙拉   dressing〔'drɛsɪŋ〕n. 調味醬
  side〔saɪd〕n. 旁邊 adj. 附加的；附帶的
  French〔frɛntʃ〕adj. 法式的
  cheese〔tʃiz〕n. 起司；乳酪   **blue cheese** 藍紋乳酪
  vinaigrette〔ˌvɪnə'grɛt〕n. 酸醬油   order〔'ɔrdɚ〕v. 點（餐）
  dish〔dɪʃ〕n. 一盤   vinegar〔'vɪnɪgɚ〕n. 醋
  vinegar salad 油醋沙拉   **side salad** 用作配菜的沙拉

42. (**B**) W: Is this movie suitable for children?

M: It's rated PG, so you can take your kids, but I wouldn't suggest it if they're very young.

W: Is there a lot of violence?

M: No. But the haunted house scene scares most kids.

Question: What type of movie is it?

A. An action film.   B. A ghost story.

C. A violent movie.   D. A cartoon.

* movie ('muvɪ) n. 電影   suitable ('sutəbḷ) adj. 適合的
rate (ret) v. 評價；認為
PG 輔導級電影 (= *parental guidance*)
kid (kɪd) n. 小孩   suggest (səg'dʒɛst) v. 建議
young (jʌŋ) adj. 年幼的   *a lot of* 很多
violence ('vaɪələns) n. 暴力
haunted ('hɔntɪd) adj. 有鬼魂出沒的
haunted house 鬼屋   scene (sin) n. 場景
scare (skɛr) v. 使驚嚇   type (taɪp) n. 類型
action ('ækʃən) n. 動作   film (fɪlm) n. 電影；影片
violent ('vaɪələnt) adj. 暴力的
cartoon (kɑr'tun) n. 卡通影片

43. (**C**) W: I hear you enjoy running.

M: I do. I run 5k nearly every morning.

W: Wow. Have you ever done a marathon?

M: Yes, but only a 10k.

Question: What did the man do?

A. He ran ten kilometers that morning.

B. He went running with his wife.

C. He competed in a ten-kilometer race.

D. He won a marathon.

* hear〔hɪr〕*v.* 聽說　　enjoy〔ɪn'dʒɔɪ〕*v.* 喜歡
run〔rʌn〕*v.* 跑步　　*5k* 五公里（= *five kilometers*）
nearly〔'nɪrlɪ〕*adv.* 幾乎　　wow〔waʊ〕*interj.* 哇；啊
do〔du〕*v.* 走過（路程）
marathon〔'mærə,θɑn〕*n.* 馬拉松
only〔'onlɪ〕*adv.* 只有　　kilometer〔'kɪlə,mitɚ〕*n.* 公里
wife〔waɪf〕*n.* 妻子　　compete〔kəm'pit〕*v.* 競爭
race〔res〕*n.* 賽跑；競賽　　win〔wɪn〕*v.* 贏

44. (**B**)　M: What a beautiful sweater! It must be by a famous designer.

W: No, actually it's handmade.

M: You made that?!

W: No, my aunt did.

Question : Where did the woman get the sweater?

A. She bought it at a famous store.

B. She received it as a gift.

C. She designed it herself.　　D. She made it.

* sweater〔'swɛtɚ〕*n.* 毛衣　　by〔baɪ〕*prep.* 由…做的
famous〔'feməs〕*adj.* 有名的
designer〔dɪ'zaɪnɚ〕*n.* 設計師
actually〔'æktʃʊəlɪ〕*adv.* 實際上
handmade〔'hænd,med〕*adj.* 手工製的
aunt〔ænt〕*n.* 阿姨　　receive〔rɪ'siv〕*v.* 收到
as〔əz, æz〕*prep.* 作爲　　gift〔gɪft〕*n.* 禮物
design〔dɪ'zaɪn〕*v.* 設計

45. (**D**) W: Did you go to the museum yesterday?

M: I did, and I really enjoyed it.

W: What impressed you the most?

M: That would have to be the dinosaur exhibit.

Question : Where did the man go?

A. An art museum.

B. An animal exhibition.

C. An impressionist show.

D. A natural history museum.

* museum〔mju'ziəm〕n. 博物館

impress〔ɪm'prɛs〕v. 使印象深刻

dinosaur〔'daɪnə,sɔr〕n. 恐龍

exhibit〔ɪg'zɪbɪt〕n. 展覽品

art〔ɑrt〕n. 藝術

art museum 美術館

animal〔'ænəmḷ〕n. 動物

exhibition〔,ɛksə'bɪʃən〕n. 展覽會

impressionist〔ɪm'prɛʃənɪst〕n. 印象派的藝術家

show〔ʃo〕n. 展示會

natural〔'nætʃərəl〕adj. 自然的

history〔'hɪstrɪ〕n. 歷史

natural history museum 自然歷史博物館

English Listening Comprehension Test

Test Book No. 8

This listening comprehension test will test your ability to understand spoken English. In this test, each conversation, statement and question will be spoken JUST ONE TIME. They will not be written out for you. There are three parts to this test. Special instructions will be given to you at the beginning of each part.

Part A

In Part A, you will see several pictures in your test book. For each picture, you will be asked 1 to 3 questions. For each question, you will hear four possible answers. Choose the best answer according to what you see in the picture.

Example:

You will see:

You will hear: What is this?

        A. This is a table.
        B. This is a chair.
        C. This is a watch.
        D. This is a doll.

The best answer to the question "What is this?" is B: "This is a chair." Therefore, you should choose answer B.

A. Questions 1-3

B. Questions 4-6

C. Questions 7-9

D. Questions 10-12

E. Question 13

F. Questions 14-15

Part B

In Part B, you will hear 15 questions. After you hear a question, read the four possible answers in your test book and decide which one is the best answer to the question you have heard.

Example:

<u>You will hear</u>: What does your father do?

<u>You will read</u>: A. He's 50 years old.

B. He's a teacher.

C. He's hungry.

D. He's in Los Angeles.

The best answer to the question "What does your father do?" is B: "He's a teacher." Therefore, you should choose answer B.

16. A. It feels cold.
    B. It's really comfortable.
    C. I think it should be cancelled.
    D. I don't trust him.

17. A. I usually eat them for breakfast.
    B. I'll have mine scrambled.
    C. I'd like two, please.
    D. No, they're not hot.

18. A. No, it was too far.

B. Yes, I spoke to him at noon.

C. No, he's too hard to teach.

D. Yes, I'll call them tonight.

19. A. I've been here for seven years.

B. I came here in the winter.

C. China is my favorite city.

D. There are better job opportunities.

20. A. Don't mention it.

B. Thanks. I'm happy about it.

C. Thank you. It's a boy.

D. Yes, they're 20 percent off.

21. A. It's my pleasure.

B. Anything to drink with that?

C. Sorry. My mistake.

D. How many orders would you like?

22. A. It's on First Street.

B. Yes, it's the best one in town.

C. No, but it's probably in the phone book.

D. How much money do you need?

23. A. Let me check his schedule.

B. Your change is twenty dollars.

C. Don't worry. He's a good doctor.

D. I'm so sorry I'm late.

24. A. Do you have a
reservation?
B. But it's already
six-thirty.
C. It's so kind of you to
invite me.
D. I had no idea it was
your birthday.

25. A. The Elephants are
the favorite.
B. It starts at seven p.m.
C. No, I don't have any
extra tickets.
D. No, I missed it, too.

26. A. Then we had better
hurry!
B. Do you want to see
the later one?
C. Yes, it finished an
hour ago.
D. Let me see if we
have any more.

27. A. That's Kim's house.
B. Look for number 232.
C. Just a deliveryman.
D. I waited only five
minutes.

28. A. Yes, I have to go and
find a book.
B. No, it's a holiday.
C. It opens for lunch in
five minutes.
D. I can't remember which
page.

29. A. I'm measuring the floor
for a new carpet.
B. The majority are
engineering students.
C. I haven't decided yet.
D. I've just started a new job.

30. A. Right away.
B. It's my treat.
C. Sure. I'll stop by.
D. As soon as the light
changes.

Part C

In Part C, you will hear 15 conversations between a man and a woman. After each conversation, you will hear a question about the conversation. After you hear the question, read the four possible answers in your test book and choose the best answer to the question you have heard.

Example:

You will hear: (Man)   How do you go to school every day?

(Woman) Usually by bus. Sometimes by taxi.

Question: How does the woman go to school?

You will read: A. She always goes to school on foot.
B. She usually rides a bike.
C. She takes either a bus or a taxi.
D. She usually goes to school by bus, never by taxi.

The best answer to the question "How does the woman go to school?" is C: "She takes either a bus or a taxi." Therefore, you should choose answer C.

31. A. She doesn't know
        Lisa.
    B. He knows the story
        is true.
    C. She should not repeat
        stories.
    D. Lisa doesn't like older
        men.

32. A. The man told her to
        get lost.
    B. There are too many
        people around.
    C. Becky likes the color
        pink.
    D. The woman is wearing
        a pink shirt, too.

33. A. It was too windy.
    B. She doesn't like
        chilies.
    C. It is unusually cold.
    D. No one turned the
        heat on.

34. A. Yes, but she will pay
        the bill.
    B. Yes, but at a later date.
    C. Yes, when she finishes
        her errands.
    D. Yes, if it rains.

35. A. She will take a taxi.
    B. She has to take two
        buses.
    C. She will drive herself
        there.
    D. She will take an airport
        bus.

36. A. Fruit for making juice.
    B. The convenience store.
    C. Around the corner.
    D. A bottle of juice.

37. A. Walking around.
    B. Looking for the MRT.
    C. Going shopping.
    D. Going for a spin.

38. A. In a clothing shop.
    B. At a tailor shop.
    C. At a dry cleaning shop.
    D. At a retail shop.

39. A. The woman has to buy something at the mall.
    B. The mall offers free parking.
    C. The woman parked illegally and got a ticket.
    D. The woman plans to buy something at the mall.

40. A. He doubts it will get cold.
    B. It is not cold now.
    C. He sees the woman is dressed too warmly.
    D. He wants to see the forecast for himself.

41. A. New York.
    B. Her office.
    C. The train station.
    D. The repair shop.

42. A. The stationery store.
    B. To buy a paper.
    C. The supply room.
    D. Her office.

43. A. In a grocery store.
    B. In an ice cream shop.
    C. In the kitchen.
    D. In a factory.

44. A. He fell off the swing.
    B. The girl pushed him.
    C. The girl let go of him.
    D. He didn't get on the swing.

45. A. A laundry.
    B. An office supply shop.
    C. A post office.
    D. A photo shop.

Listening Test 8 詳解

Part A

For questions number 1 to 3, please look at picture A.

1. (**B**) What do the cats think of Hello Kitty?
   A. They think she is not a cat.
   B. They like her very much.
   C. They are hungry.　　D. There are four cats.

   * like〔laɪk〕v. 喜歡　　hungry〔'hʌŋgrɪ〕adj. 飢餓的

2. (**A**) Please look at picture A again. What is behind Hello Kitty?
   A. An unhappy cat.　　B. Three cats.
   C. A box.　　D. A bow.

   * behind〔bɪ'haɪnd〕prep. 在…後面
   unhappy〔ʌn'hæpɪ〕adj. 不高興的
   box〔bɑks〕n. 箱子　　bow〔bo〕n. 蝴蝶結

3. (**D**) Please look at picture A again. How does Hello Kitty look?
   A. Lovely.　　B. Lonely.
   C. Angry.　　D. Dirty.

   * look〔luk〕v. 看起來　　lovely〔'lʌvlɪ〕adj. 可愛的
   lonely〔'lonlɪ〕adj. 寂寞的
   angry〔'æŋgrɪ〕adj. 生氣的　　dirty〔'dɜtɪ〕adj. 髒的

For questions number 4 to 6, please look at picture B.

4. (**C**) What is the man holding?

A. He is scratching.　　B. He is hot.

C. It's a wig.　　D. On a chair.

* hold〔hold〕v. 拿著

scratch〔skrætʃ〕v. 搔（癢）　hot〔hɑt〕adj. 熱的

wig〔wɪg〕n. 假髮

5. (**B**) Please look at picture B again. Who is in the picture on the wall?

A. An old man.

B. A young man.

C. Her father.

D. A movie star.

* picture〔'pɪktʃɚ〕n. 照片　wall〔wɔl〕n. 牆壁

young〔jʌŋ〕adj. 年輕的　movie〔'muvɪ〕n. 電影

star〔stɑr〕n. 明星

6. (**A**) Please look at picture B again. How does the girl feel?

A. Shocked.　　B. Excited.

C. Hungry.　　D. Smashed.

* feel〔fil〕v. 覺得　shocked〔ʃɑkt〕adj. 震驚的

excited〔ɪk'saɪtɪd〕adj. 興奮的

smashed〔smæʃt〕adj. 酒醉的

For questions number 7 to 9, please look at picture C.

7. (**D**) What is the girl doing?

   A. She is waiting for the boy.

   B. She is cooking.

   C. She is dieting.

   D. She is eating.

   * **wait for** 等候　　cook〔kʊk〕v. 煮；烹飪
     diet〔'daɪət〕v. 節食

8. (**C**) Please look at picture C again. What did the boy bring?

   A. Surprised.　　　　　B. Chicken.

   C. Flowers.　　　　　　D. A picture.

   * bring〔brɪŋ〕v. 帶來
     surprised〔sə'praɪzd〕adj. 驚訝的
     chicken〔'tʃɪkɪn〕n. 雞肉　　flower〔'flaʊə〕n. 花
     picture〔'pɪktʃə〕n. 照片；畫

9. (**B**) Please look at picture C again. What is on the middle plate?

   A. Chicken.　　　　　　B. Bread.

   C. Fruit.　　　　　　　D. Juice.

   * middle〔'mɪdl̩〕adj. 中間的　　plate〔plet〕n. 盤子
     bread〔brɛd〕n. 麵包　　fruit〔frut〕n. 水果
     juice〔dʒus〕n. 果汁

For questions number 10 to 12, please look at picture D.

10. (**C**) What is in the ice?

      A. A fish.   B. A penguin.

      C. A hole.   D. A stick.

      * ice 〔 aɪs 〕 *n.* 冰   fish 〔 fɪʃ 〕 *n.* 魚

       penguin 〔 'pɛngwɪn 〕 *n.* 企鵝

       hole 〔 hol 〕 *n.* 洞   stick 〔 stɪk 〕 *n.* 棍子

11. (**A**) Please look at picture D again. What is the penguin
      doing?

      A. Fishing.   B. Swimming.

      C. Asking.   D. Giving.

      * fish 〔 fɪʃ 〕 *v.* 釣魚   swim 〔 swɪm 〕 *v.* 游泳

12. (**D**) Please look at picture D again. Why is the penguin
      doing this?

      A. He is hungry.

      B. He wants to win a contest.

      C. He is lovely.

      D. He wants to have a girlfriend.

      * win 〔 wɪn 〕 *v.* 贏得

       contest 〔 'kɑntɛst 〕 *n.* 比賽

       lovely 〔 'lʌvlɪ 〕 *adj.* 可愛的

       girlfriend 〔 'gɝl,frɛnd 〕 *n.* 女朋友

For question number 13, please look at picture E.

13.(**C**) What is on the chest?

A. Her hair.　　　　　　B. A dress.

C. A fan.　　　　　　　D. A drawer.

* chest (tʃɛst) *n.* 衣櫃　　hair (hɛr) *n.* 頭髮

dress (drɛs) *n.* 洋裝　　fan (fæn) *n.* 風扇

drawer (drɔr) *n.* 抽屜

For questions number 14 and 15, please look at picture F.

14.(**D**) What is the girl doing?

A. Drawing.

B. Dropping a cigarette.

C. Washing the window.

D. Looking at the moon.

* draw (drɔ) *v.* 畫畫　　drop (drɑp) *v.* 使掉落

cigarette ('sɪgə,rɛt) *n.* 香菸　　wash (wɑʃ) *v.* 清洗

window ('wɪndo) *n.* 窗戶　　*look at* 看

moon (mun) *n.* 月亮

15.(**A**) Please look at picture F again. Where is she?

A. She is in a city.　　B. She is sad.

C. She is a girlfriend.　　D. She is outside.

* city ('sɪtɪ) *n.* 城市

sad (sæd) *adj.* 難過的；悲傷的

outside ('aʊt'saɪd) *adv.* 在外面

Part B

16. (**D**) What's your feeling about the candidate?

　　　A. It feels cold. 　　　　B. It's really comfortable.

　　　C. I think it should be cancelled.

　　　D. I don't trust him.

　　　＊ feeling〔'filɪŋ〕 n. 感覺　　candidate〔'kændə,det〕 n. 候選人
　　　　feel〔fil〕 v. 使人感覺　　cold〔kold〕 adj. 寒冷的
　　　　comfortable〔'kʌmfə·təbḷ〕 adj. 舒適的
　　　　cancel〔'kænsḷ〕 v. 取消　　trust〔trʌst〕 v. 信任

17. (**B**) How do you like your eggs?

　　　A. I usually eat them for breakfast.

　　　B. I'll have mine scrambled.

　　　C. I'd like two, please. 　　D. No, they're not hot.

　　　＊ *How do you like your egg?* 你的蛋想要怎麼煮？
　　　　usually〔'juʒʊəlɪ〕 adv. 通常
　　　　scramble〔'skræmbḷ〕 v. 炒（蛋）　　*would like* 想要

18. (**B**) Were you able to reach David today?

　　　A. No, it was too far.

　　　B. Yes, I spoke to him at noon.

　　　C. No, he's too hard to teach.

　　　D. Yes, I'll call them tonight.

　　　＊ *be able to V.* 能夠⋯　　reach〔ritʃ〕 v. 連絡
　　　　David〔'devɪd〕 n. 大衛　　far〔fɑr〕 adj. 遠的
　　　　noon〔nun〕 n. 中午　　*too⋯to~* 太⋯以致於不能~
　　　　hard〔hɑrd〕 adj. 困難的　　teach〔titʃ〕 v. 教
　　　　call〔kɔl〕 v. 打電話給

19. (**D**) For what reason did you move to the city?

A. I've been here for seven years.

B. I came here in the winter.

C. China is my favorite city.

D. There are better job opportunities.

* reason〔ˋrizn̩〕 n. 原因;理由
  move〔muv〕 v. 搬家　city〔ˋsɪtɪ〕 n. 城市
  winter〔ˋwɪntɚ〕 n. 冬天　China〔ˋtʃaɪnə〕 n. 中國
  favorite〔ˋfevərɪt〕 adj. 最喜歡的
  job〔dʒɑb〕 n. 工作
  opportunity〔͵ɑpɚˋtjunətɪ〕 n. 機會

20. (**B**) Congratulations on your promotion!

A. Don't mention it.

B. Thanks. I'm happy about it.

C. Thank you. It's a boy.

D. Yes, they're 20 percent off.

* congratulations〔kən͵grætʃəˋleʃənz〕 n. pl. 恭喜
  promotion〔prəˋmoʃən〕 n. 升遷
  Don't mention it. 別客氣。
  percent〔pɚˋsɛnt〕 adj. 百分之…的
  20 percent off 打八折

21. (**C**) I didn't order this.

A. It's my pleasure.

B. Anything to drink with that?

C. Sorry. My mistake.

D. How many orders would you like?

* order (ˈɔrdɚ) v. 點 (餐) n. 一份 (餐點)
pleasure (ˈplɛʒɚ) n. 榮幸
It's my pleasure. 這是我的榮幸。
mistake (məˈstek) n. 錯誤

22. (**C**) Do you know the number of the bank?

A. It's on First Street.

B. Yes, it's the best one in town.

C. No, but it's probably in the phone book.

D. How much money do you need?

* number (ˈnʌmbɚ) n. 電話號碼   bank (bæŋk) n. 銀行
town (taʊn) n. 城鎮   probably (ˈprɑbəblɪ) adv. 可能
phone book 電話簿   need (nid) v. 需要

23. (**A**) I wonder if I could change my appointment with Dr. Lee.

A. Let me check his schedule.

B. Your change is twenty dollars.

C. Don't worry. He's a good doctor.

D. I'm so sorry I'm late.

* wonder (ˈwʌndɚ) v. 想知道   if (ɪf) conj. 是否
change (tʃendʒ) v. 變更   n. 找的零錢
appointment (əˈpɔɪntmənt) n. (訪問、診療等的) 約會；預約
Dr. (ˈdɑktɚ) n. …醫師   Lee (li) n. 李
check (tʃɛk) v. 檢查；確認
schedule (ˈskɛdʒul) n. 時間表
worry (ˈwɝɪ) v. 擔心   late (let) adj. 遲到的

24. (**A**) We'd like a table for a party of six, please.

    A. Do you have a reservation?

    B. But it's already six-thirty.

    C. It's so kind of you to invite me.

    D. I had no idea it was your birthday.

    * **would like** 想要

        party ('partɪ) n. 一行人;一夥人

        reservation (ˌrɛzəˈveʃən) n. 預訂

        already (ɔlˈrɛdɪ) adv. 已經

        kind (kaɪnd) adj. 好心的;親切的

        invite (ɪnˈvaɪt) v. 邀請

        I have no idea… 我不知道…

        birthday ('bɝθˌde) n. 生日

25. (**D**) Do you know who won the game last night?

    A. The Elephants are the favorite.

    B. It starts at seven p.m.

    C. No, I don't have any extra tickets.

    D. No, I missed it, too.

    * win (wɪn) v. 贏得   game (gem) n. 比賽

        elephant ('ɛləfənt) n. 大象

        favorite ('fevərɪt) n. 最受喜愛的人或物

        start (start) v. 開始

        p.m. ('pi'ɛm) adv. 下午 (= pm = P.M. = PM)

        extra ('ɛkstrə) adj. 額外的

        ticket ('tɪkɪt) n. 票;入場券   miss (mɪs) v. 錯過

26. (**B**) I'm afraid the three-thirty show is sold out.

    A. Then we had better hurry!

    B. Do you want to see the later one?

    C. Yes, it finished an hour ago.

    D. Let me see if we have any more.

    * afraid〔ə'fred〕*adj.* 恐怕…的

      show〔ʃo〕*n.* 電影

      sold out 售完   *had better V.* 最好~

      hurry〔'hɜɪ〕*v.* 趕快   later〔'letæ〕*adj.* 較晚的

      finish〔'fɪnɪʃ〕*v.* 結束

      more〔mor〕*adj.* 多餘的；另外的

27. (**C**) Who was at the door?

    A. That's Kim's house.

    B. Look for number 232.

    C. Just a deliveryman.

    D. I waited only five minutes.

    * *at the door* 在門口   Kim〔kɪm〕*n.* 金恩

      look for 尋找   number〔'nʌmbæ〕*n.* 第…號

      just〔dʒʌst〕*adv.* 只是

      deliveryman〔dɪ'lɪvərɪˌmæn〕*n.* 送貨員

      wait〔wet〕*v.* 等   minute〔'mɪnɪt〕*n.* 分鐘

28. (**B**) Was the library open today?

    A. Yes, I have to go and find a book.

    B. No, it's a holiday.

C. It opens for lunch in five minutes.

D. I can't remember which page.

* library〔'laɪ,brɛrɪ〕 n. 圖書館
open〔'opən〕 adj. 開著的　v. 開門；開始營業
holiday〔'halə,de〕 n. 假日
remember〔rɪ'mɛmbɚ〕 v. 記得
which〔hwɪtʃ〕 pron. 哪一個　　page〔pedʒ〕 n. 頁

29. (**C**) What are you majoring in?

A. I'm measuring the floor for a new carpet.

B. The majority are engineering students.

C. I haven't decided yet.

D. I've just started a new job.

* major〔'medʒɚ〕 v. 主修＜ in ＞　measure〔'mɛʒɚ〕 v. 測量
floor〔flor〕 n. 地板　　carpet〔'karpɪt〕 n. 地毯
majority〔mə'dʒɔrətɪ〕 n. 大多數
engineering〔,ɛndʒə'nɪrɪŋ〕 n. 工程學
decide〔dɪ'saɪd〕 v. 決定　　**not…yet** 尚未…
start〔start〕 v. 開始　　job〔dʒab〕 n. 工作

30. (**A**) Bring us another round, please.

A. Right away.　　　　B. It's my treat.

C. Sure. I'll stop by.　　D. As soon as the light changes.

* bring〔brɪŋ〕 v. 帶來　　another〔ə'nʌðɚ〕 adj. 另一個
round〔raʊnd〕 n. （酒的）全體喝一巡（的份量）
Right away. 馬上來。　　treat〔trit〕 n. 請客
It's my treat. 我請客。　　**stop by** 順道拜訪
as soon as 一…就…　　light〔laɪt〕 n. 燈
change〔tʃendʒ〕 v. 改變

Part C

31. (**C**) W: Hey, did you hear about Lisa?

M: No. What happened?

W: I heard she broke up with Brian. And now she's dating some older guy.

M: You don't know if that's true. You really shouldn't gossip about people.

Question : What does the man say to the woman?

A. She doesn't know Lisa.
B. He knows the story is true.
C. She should not repeat stories.
D. Lisa doesn't like older men.

* hey〔he〕*interj.* 嘿
  hear about 聽到⋯的消息
  Lisa〔'lisə〕*n.* 莉莎
  happen〔'hæpən〕*v.* 發生
  break up with sb. 和某人分手
  Brian〔'braɪən〕*n.* 布萊恩
  date〔det〕*v.* 和⋯約會　　some〔sʌm〕*adv.* 某個
  guy〔gaɪ〕*n.*（男）人；傢伙
  if〔ɪf〕*conj.* 是否　　true〔tru〕*adj.* 真實的
  gossip〔'gasəp〕*v.* 說閒話
  repeat〔rɪ'pit〕*v.* 重複；向別人轉述
  story〔'storɪ〕*n.* 故事；傳聞

32. (**B**) M : Can you see Becky? I've lost her in the crowd.

   W : No. What color shirt is she wearing?

   M : She has on a pink shirt.

   W : That's no help. Most of the girls here are wearing pink.

   Question : Why can't they see Becky?

   A. The man told her to get lost.

   B. There are too many people around.

   C. Becky likes the color pink.

   D. The woman is wearing a pink shirt, too.

   * Becky ('bɛkɪ) *n.* 貝琪

   lose (luz) *v.* 失去

   crowd (kraʊd) *n.* 人群；群眾

   color ('kʌlə) *n.* 顏色　　shirt (ʃɜt) *n.* 襯衫

   wear (wɛr) *v.* 穿著

   pink (pɪŋk) *adj.* 粉紅色的　*n.* 粉紅色

   help (hɛlp) *n.* 幫助

   She has on a pink shirt. 她穿著粉紅色的襯衫。

   　(= *She has a pink shirt on.* = *She is wearing a pink shirt.*)

   most of the~ 大部分的~　　***get lost*** 滾開

   around (ə'raʊnd) *adv.* 在周圍

   like (laɪk) *v.* 喜歡

33. (**A**) W : Would you close the window, please? It's a bit chilly.

   M : No problem. Do you want me to turn the heat on?

W: No, that's not necessary. I think it was the draft that was bothering me.

M: Probably. It's really not that cold out yet.

Question : Why was the woman uncomfortable?

A. It was too windy.

B. She doesn't like chilies.

C. It is unusually cold.

D. No one turned the heat on.

* close〔kloz〕v. 關上
window〔'wɪndo〕n. 窗戶
a bit 有點　　chilly〔'tʃɪlɪ〕adj. 寒冷的
turn on 打開（電器）　　heat〔hit〕n. 暖氣
necessary〔'nɛsə͵sɛrɪ〕adj. 必要的
draft〔dræft〕n. 穿堂風；一陣風
bother〔'baðɚ〕v. 使困擾
probably〔'prabəblɪ〕adv. 可能
cold〔kold〕adj. 冷的　　out〔aut〕adv. 外面
yet〔jɛt〕adv. 尚（未）
uncomfortable〔ʌn'kʌmfɚtəbḷ〕adj. 不舒服的
windy〔'wɪndɪ〕adj. 風大的
chili〔'tʃɪlɪ〕n. 紅番椒
unusually〔ʌn'juʒʊəlɪ〕adv. 異常地

34. (**B**) M: What are you doing for lunch?

W: I've got a lot of errands to run, so I'll probably just get some take away.

M: Too bad. I was going to treat you to lunch at the new restaurant across the street.

W: I'll take a rain check.

Question : Will the woman go to lunch with the man?

A. Yes, but she will pay the bill.

B. Yes, but at a later date.

C. Yes, when she finishes her errands.

D. Yes, if it rains.

* *I've got* 我有　　*a lot of* 很多　　errand (ˈɛrənd) *n.* 差事
run (rʌn) *v.* 跑腿　　get (gɛt) *v.* 買
take away 外帶食物 (= *take out*)
bad (bæd) *adj.* 可惜的　　*treat sb. to ~* 請某人吃~
restaurant (ˈrɛstərənt) *n.* 餐廳
across the street 在對街　　*rain check* 改天再招待
pay (pe) *v.* 支付；付 (錢)　　bill (bɪl) *n.* 帳單
later (ˈletɚ) *adj.* 較晚的　　date (det) *n.* 日期
finish (ˈfɪnɪʃ) *v.* 完成；結束　　rain (ren) *v.* 下雨

35. (**D**) W: Do you know if I can get a bus to the airport here?

M: If you go from here, you'll have to change buses. But there's an airport bus stop a few blocks away.

W: I have so much to carry by myself. I guess I could take a taxi to the bus stop.

Question : How will the woman get to the airport?

A. She will take a taxi.

B. She has to take two buses.

C. She will drive herself there.

D. She will take an airport bus.

* airport ('ɛr,port) n. 機場　change (tʃendʒ) v. 更換
stop (stɑp) n. 候車站；停車站　a few 一些
block (blɑk) n. 街區　away (ə'we) adv. 遠
carry ('kærɪ) v. 拿；提　by oneself 獨自
guess (gɛs) v. 猜　get to 到達　take (tek) v. 搭乘
taxi ('tæksɪ) n. 計程車　drive (draɪv) v. 開車載

36. (**D**)　M : Is there a supermarket near here?

W : No, there isn't. But there is a convenience store
around the corner.

M : I guess that will do. I just want to get some juice
or fresh fruit.

W : They'll have juice, but it will be a little more
expensive.

Question : What will the man buy?

A. Fruit for making juice.　B. The convenience store.

C. Around the corner.　D. A bottle of juice.

* supermarket ('supə,mɑrkɪt) n. 超級市場
near (nɪr) prep. 在…附近
convenience (kən'vinjəns) n. 便利；方便
convenience store 便利商店　corner ('kɔrnə) n. 轉角
around the corner 在轉角　do (du) v. 可以
get (gɛt) v. 買　juice (dʒus) n. 果汁
fresh (frɛʃ) adj. 新鮮的　fruit (frut) n. 水果
a little 有點　expensive (ɪk'spɛnsɪv) adj. 昂貴的
make (mek) v. 製作　bottle ('bɑtḷ) n. 瓶；一瓶的量

37. (**C**) W: I'm turned around. Which exit should I take for Sogo Department Store?

M: Go out exit 2, and you'll see the store ahead of you on the left.

W: Thanks. I never know where I am in these MRT stations.

M: It can be confusing.

Question : What is the woman doing today?

A. Walking around.

B. Looking for the MRT.

C. Going shopping.

D. Going for a spin.

* ***I'm turned around.*** 我不知該往哪裡走;我迷失了方向。

(= *I don't know which direction to go.* = *I've lost my sense of direction.*)

exit〔'ɛgzɪt,'ɛksɪt〕*n.* 出口   take〔tek〕*v.* 選擇

department store 百貨公司   ***go out*** 從 (…門) 出去

ahead of 在…前面   left〔lɛft〕*n.* 左邊

never〔'nɛvɚ〕*adv.* 從未;絕不

MRT 大眾捷運系統 (= *Mass Rapid Transit*)

MRT station 捷運車站

confusing〔kən'fjuzɪŋ〕*adj.* 令人迷惑的

walk around 閒晃   ***look for*** 尋找

shop〔ʃɑp〕*v.* 購物

spin〔spɪn〕*n.* 旋轉;跑一圈;跑一趟

go for a spin 去兜一圈

38. (**C**) M: Hi. Can you have these clothes ready by tomorrow?

W: No problem.

M: There is a stain on this jacket that may need special attention.

W: I see. I'll do my best, but I can't promise that that will come out.

Question : Where does this conversation take place?

A. In a clothing shop.
B. At a tailor shop.
C. At a dry cleaning shop.
D. At a retail shop.

* clothes〔kloz〕 *n. pl.* 衣服　　ready〔'rɛdɪ〕 *adj.* 準備好的
by〔baɪ〕 *prep.* 在⋯之前　　stain〔sten〕 *n.* 污跡
jacket〔'dʒækɪt〕 *n.* 夾克　　special〔'spɛʃəl〕 *adj.* 特別的
attention〔ə'tɛnʃən〕 *n.* 注意　　***do one's best*** 盡力
promise〔'pramɪs〕 *v.* 保證；承諾
come out（污跡）消除
conversation〔ˌkɑnvɚ'seʃən〕 *n.* 對話
take place 發生　　clothing〔'kloðɪŋ〕 *n.* 衣服
tailor〔'telɚ〕 *n.* 裁縫師　　***tailor shop*** 裁縫店
dry cleaning shop 乾洗店　　retail〔'ritel〕 *n.* 零售

39. (**D**) W: I can't believe we have to pay for parking at the mall!

M: Don't worry about it. You're bound to buy something.

W: That's what I mean. Why should I have to pay to park when I'm buying something from them?

M: But when you buy something, you can get the parking ticket validated. Then you don't pay, see?

Question : What is true?

A. The woman has to buy something at the mall.

B. The mall offers free parking.

C. The woman parked illegally and got a ticket.

D. The woman plans to buy something at the mall.

* believe〔bɪ'liv〕v. 相信　*pay for* 付～的錢
　park〔pɑrk〕v. 停車　mall〔mɔl〕n. 購物中心
　be bound to V. 一定會…　mean〔min〕v. 意思是
　ticket〔'tɪkɪt〕n. 票；券；罰單
　validate〔'vælə,det〕v. 使有效　*See?* 了解了嗎？
　true〔tru〕adj. 真實的；正確的　offer〔'ɔfɚ〕v. 提供
　free〔fri〕adj. 免費的　illegally〔ɪ'liglɪ〕adv. 違法地
　plan〔plæn〕v. 計畫

40. (**A**)　M: Why are you dressed so warmly? It's nearly 30
　　　　　degrees!

W: Didn't you see the forecast? It's supposed to get
　cold tonight.

M: I'll believe that when I see it.

Question : What does the man mean?

A. He doubts it will get cold.　　B. It is not cold now.

C. He sees the woman is dressed too warmly.

D. He wants to see the forecast for himself.

* dress〔drɛs〕v. 使穿衣服　warmly〔'wɔrmlɪ〕adj. 溫暖地
　nearly〔'nɪrlɪ〕adv. 將近　degree〔dɪ'gri〕n. 度
　forecast〔'for,kæst〕n. 預報　*be supposed to V.* 應該～
　cold〔kold〕adj. 寒冷的　*get cold* 變冷
　doubt〔daʊt〕v. 懷疑　*for* oneself 親自

41. (**B**) W: Can you give me a lift to work today?

M: What's wrong with your car?

W: Nothing. I'm taking a train to New York after work tonight, and I'd rather not leave my car in the city.

M: No problem.

Question : Where does the woman want to go now?

A. New York.   B. Her office.

C. The train station.   D. The repair shop.

* lift〔lıft〕n. 搭便車
  give sb. a lift 載某人一程；讓某人搭便車
  What's wrong with～? ～怎麼了？
  train〔tren〕n. 火車   ***New York*** 紐約
  after work 下班之後   ***would rather*** 寧願
  leave〔liv〕v. 留下   city〔'sıtı〕n. 城市
  office〔'ɔfıs〕n. 辦公室；公司   ***train station*** 火車站
  repair〔rı'pɛr〕v. n. 修理   ***repair shop*** 修理廠

42. (**C**) M: Could you pick up some more printer paper for me when you go downstairs?

W: Sure, but I'll have to put your name on the requisition form. I've already taken two packs of paper for myself this month.

M: Do they really care how much paper we use?

W: The company cares if they think we are wasting supplies.

Question : Where is the woman going?

A. The stationery store.　B. To buy a paper.
C. The supply room.　D. Her office.

* ***pick up*** 拿　printer (ˈprɪntɚ) n. 印表機
downstairs (ˈdaʊnˈstɛrz) adv. 到樓下　***go downstairs*** 下樓
requisition (ˌrɛkwəˈzɪʃən) n. 需要；申請領取單
form (fɔrm) n. 表格　already (ɔlˈrɛdɪ) adv. 已經
pack (pæk) n. 一包　company (ˈkʌmpənɪ) n. 公司
care (kɛr) v. 關心；在乎　waste (west) v. 浪費
supplies (səˈplaɪz) n. pl. 供應品；儲備物資
stationery store 文具店　***supply room*** 供應室

43. (**B**) W: What flavor would you like?
M: I can't decide between the Very Berry and the
　Chocolate Delight.
W: You can taste them first if you like.
M: Never mind. I'll just have one scoop of each, and
　a coffee, please.

Question : Where are the speakers?

A. In a grocery store.　B. In an ice cream shop.
C. In the kitchen.　D. In a factory.

* flavor (ˈflevɚ) n. 口味；味道　decide (dɪˈsaɪd) v. 決定
between (bəˈtwin) prep. 在 (兩者) 之間
berry (ˈbɛrɪ) n. 漿果；莓　chocolate (ˈtʃɔklɪt) n. 巧克力
delight (dɪˈlaɪt) n. 歡喜；喜悅　taste (test) v. 品嚐
never mind 算了；沒關係　scoop (skup) n. 一舀；一杓
coffee (ˈkɔfɪ) n. 咖啡　speaker (ˈspikɚ) n. 說話者
grocery (ˈgrosərɪ) n. 食品雜貨
grocery store 雜貨店　***ice cream*** 冰淇淋
kitchen (ˈkɪtʃɪn) n. 廚房　factory (ˈfæktrɪ) n. 工廠

44. (**A**) M : Why is Billy crying?

W : He fell down.

M : How did that happen?

W : I was pushing him on the swing and he didn't hold on tight.

Question : How did Billy fall?

A. He fell off the swing.　　B. The girl pushed him.

C. The girl let go of him.

D. He didn't get on the swing.

* ***fall down*** 跌落　　push〔puʃ〕v. 推

swing〔swɪŋ〕n. 鞦韆　　tight〔taɪt〕adv. 緊緊地

hold on tight 抓緊　　fall〔fɔl〕v. 跌落

fall off 跌落　　***let go of*** 放開…　　***get on*** 坐上；登上

45. (**D**) W : Do you know what time the shop opens?

M : I think it opens at 10:00.

W : Oh, no! That's too late. I need to pick up my pictures before work today.

M : You could call them after ten and see if they'll deliver them to your office.

Question : What kind of shop is it?

A. A laundry.　　　　　B. An office supply shop.

C. A post office.　　　　D. A photo shop.

* open〔'opən〕v. 營業　　late〔let〕adj. 遲的；晚的

pick up 拿　　deliver〔dɪ'lɪvɚ〕v. 遞送

kind〔kaɪnd〕n. 種類　　laundry〔'lɔndrɪ〕n. 洗衣店

office supply shop 辦公室用品店　　photo〔'foto〕n. 照片

劉毅英文「中級英檢保證班」

　　對於國中生來說，考上「初檢」已經沒有什麼稀奇，唯有在國二、國三考過「中級英檢」，才高人一等。有這張「中級英檢」證書，有助於申請高中入學，或高中語文資優班。

I. 上課時間：台中總部：每週六晚上6：00～9：00
　　　　　　台北本部：每週日晚上6：30～9：30

II. 上課方式：完全比照最新「中檢」命題標準命題，我們將新編的試題，印成一整本，讓同學閱讀複習方便。老師視情況上課，讓同學做測驗，同學不需要交卷，老師立刻講解，一次一次地訓練，讓同學輕鬆取得認證。

III. 保證辦法：同學只要報一次名，就可以終生上課，考上為止，但必須每年至少考一次「中級英檢」，憑成績單才可以繼續上課，否則就必須重新報名，才能再上課。報名參加「中級英檢測驗」，但缺考，則視同沒有報名。

IV. 報名贈書：1.中級英檢公佈字彙
　　　　　　2.中級英語字彙500題（價值180元）
　　　　　　3.中級英語克漏字測驗（價值180元）
　　　　　　4.中級英語文法測驗（價值180元）
　　　　　　5.中級英語閱讀測驗（價值180元）
　　　　　　6.中級英語聽力測驗（書＋CD一套（價值680元）
　　　　　　【贈書將視實際情況調整】

V. 上課教材：

VI. 報名地點：台中總部：台中市三民路三段125號7F（李卓澔數學樓上）
　　　　　　TEL：（04）2221-8861

　　　　　　台北本部：台北市許昌街17號6F（火車站前・壽德大樓）
　　　　　　TEL：（02）2389-5212

劉毅英文「中高級英檢保證班」

高中同學通過「中級檢定」已經沒什麼用了，因為這個證書本來就應該得到。你應該參加「中高級英檢」認證考試，有了這張證書，對你甄試申請入學，有很大的幫助。愈早考完，就顯示你愈優秀。

I. 上課時間：A班：每週二晚上6：30～9：30
　　　　　　B班：每週日下午2：00～5：00
　　　　　　※每年開課2期，上課日期以實際公告為準。

　　　　　　▶同學可以選一班上課，也可兩班同時上課，隨時報名，立即上課。

II. 上課方式：初試課程 完全比照財團法人語言訓練中心的「中高級英檢初試」的題型命題。一回試題包括45題聽力測驗，50題閱讀能力測驗，我們將新編的試題，印成一整本，讓同學閱讀複習方便。老師視情況上課，讓同學做聽力測驗或閱讀測驗，同學不需要交卷，老師立刻講解閱讀能力測驗部份，聽力部份則發放詳解，讓同學回家加強演練，全面提升答題技巧。

　　　　　　複試課程 完全比照全真「中高級複試」命題標準命題，我們將新編的試題，印成一整本，以便複習，老師分析試題，一次一次地訓練，讓同學輕鬆取得認證。

III. 收費標準：14,800元（贈送代辦報名費初試和複試各一次，價值2,000元，本班幫同學代辦報名）
　　　　　　※一次繳費，直到考取認證為止！

IV. 保證辦法：同學只要報一次名，就可以終生上課，考上為止，但必須每年至少考一次「中高級英檢」，憑成績單才可以繼續上課，否則就必須重新報名，才能再上課。報名參加「中高級英檢測驗」，但缺考，則視同沒有報名。

V. 報名贈書：1.中高級英檢1000字（價值220元）
　　　　　　2.中高級英語克漏字測驗（價值280元）
　　　　　　3.中高級英語閱讀測驗（價值280元）
　　　　　　4.中高級英文法480題（價值220元）
　　　　　　5.中高級英語聽力檢定（書＋CD一套）（價值720元）
　　　　　　6.中高級口說全模擬實戰題庫（價值250元）

VI. 上課教材：

VII. 報名地點：台北市許昌街17號6F（火車站前・壽德大樓）
　　　　　　TEL：（02）2389-5212

中級英語聽力檢定⑦

主　　　編 / 劉　毅

發　行　所 / 學習出版有限公司　　　☎ (02) 2704-5525

郵 撥 帳 號 / 0512727-2 學習出版社帳戶

登　記　證 / 局版台業 *2179* 號

印　刷　所 / 裕強彩色印刷有限公司

台 北 門 市 / 台北市許昌街 10 號 2 F　　☎ (02) 2331-4060・2331-9209

台灣總經銷 / 紅螞蟻圖書有限公司　　　☎ (02) 2795-3656

美國總經銷 / Evergreen Book Store　　☎ (818) 2813622

本公司網址　www.learnbook.com.tw

電 子 郵 件　learnbook@learnbook.com.tw

書＋MP3 一片售價：新台幣二百八十元正

2008 年 12 月 1 日初版

ISBN 978-986-231-010-6